The Shattered People

The Shattered People

ROBERT HOSKINS

DOUBLEDAY & COMPANY, INC.

GARDEN CITY, NEW YORK

1975

All of the characters in this book
are fictitious, and any resemblance
to actual persons, living or dead,
is purely coincidental.

Library of Congress Cataloging in Publication Data

Hoskins, Robert.
    The shattered people.

    I. Title.
PZ4.H828Sh [PS3558.076]   813'.5'4
ISBN 0-385-09934-7
Library of Congress Catalog Card Number 74-24487

For Sarah Irene Clune, my mother

The Shattered People

CHAPTER ONE

Aaron crouched deeper into the tall grass at the edge of the shallow draw. A narrow clay beach opposite his position was muddy and well trampled, the smell of water sweet on the early evening air. The block of rough salt he had placed earlier that day, digging a firm setting in the clay a double arm's length above the beach, was already attracting the first thirst slakers of the evening.

They were little, though, and even as his eye sized them carefully and his right hand balanced the egg-shaped rock in the pocket of the sling, he knew they were not worth the effort of taking. He watched them for a time as they darted to the edge of the spring-fed pool to dip cautious tongues barely far enough into the biting-cold water to wet them, then scurried for the other treasure that tantalized. Overcome with excitement by the unexpected riches, the little ones chased back and forth in frantic confusion.

Aaron watched one of the scurriers with mild interest, one corner of his mind considering how he might take it. He would have to be several days farther toward starvation before he would put the plan into action—a single swallow of life-liquid, a few shreds of tissue, energy for the last extremity and no more. But he was a hunter by nature and a hunter by appointment, and it was his fashion to consider the mechanics of the hunt at every opportunity.

He was waiting now for the larger game that would come to the waterhole with evening—there was ample evidence of their activity, and even well-defined trails. But he was not yet ready to waste energy on backtracking a beast which might not be where he expected it to be. The salt lick was inducement enough to insure that there would be no shortage of targets, and should further cause them to lose at least some of their natural caution. The salt piece had been carefully pried from the outcropping near the village—nearly a hundred miles away from here, across the desert—and had been immediately wrapped in several layers of pungent leaf to insure that there would be no man-spoor to contaminate it. After planting the salt in the hole in the clay bank, Aaron had dragged desert brush behind him to eliminate his trail. His waiting place had been chosen only after careful consideration of the winds that swept erratically across this corner of the plain.

Now dusk was at hand. Soon his wait would be over.

The watcher in the tall grass was naked, body burned a deep bronze-red by long days under the sun that baked the desert and the neighboring plains. A generous coating of summer dust was streaked by sweat runnels, giving him a painted appearance. A pliable length of grass bound long bleached hair back from his eyes; another about his waist held an open leather wallet. That, with the sling, was the only evidence of artifact.

His face was as beardless as a youth's, though his forehead was lined with the faint wrinkles of marching age, telling that his body had seen the planetary orbits of three youth-times. At the moment his entire body was covered with light scratches and minor welts, from where he had forced a path through the thorny underbrush to his waiting place, a path chosen to let him avoid the game trails.

The hours passed slowly, the watching man not moving from his position beyond an occasion flick of tongue to remove a sweat beadlet from his lips. A large mud rutter appeared once, stirring his interest until he spotted the thickening of armored protection on back and neck, proof against anything so casual as his sling.

After a time that might have been hours, and just as the day was about to fade completely under a rising curtain of blazing stars, Aaron's patience was rewarded. A massive browser poked broad curving horns over the far edge of the draw.

The creature was immediately opposite Aaron. His muscles tensed as it surveyed the scene around the waterhole, casting its eyes about suspiciously and sniffing the air with every slight shift of the now-gentle breeze. But Aaron had chosen his spot well; the quarry could not locate his spoor and did not pick him out from the background of the thick underbrush.

The man waited until it was halfway down the path, beyond safe retreat and cut off by distance from escaping out the gentler slopes that led up and out of the ends of the draw. Then a scream burst from Aaron's lips, a cry of supreme confidence.

The creature stumbled, surprised, and lost its footing. It began to slip down the slippery clay of the bank, eyes flaring so large with fear that Aaron could see the blaze of its pupils. Then one forefoot found unexpected purchase on a protrusion of rock, and it wheeled about to flee back up the side of the bank.

Aaron stood and in one fluid movement let fly with his sling. The path of the missile was straight and sure and the beast's head slammed against the bank before it had gained a yard, skull smashed. It hung there, pinned motionless for an instant of frozen time, then began to slip downward. A rear leg buckled and it began to tumble, rolling end over end down the path until it flopped onto the muddy clay of the little beach, hind quarters slapping into the water of the pool.

A small avalanche of stones rattled around the still-quivering body, the only noise for a span of seconds; and then the beach suddenly emptied of all other forms of life, the drinkers seeking cover in grass, brush, and even in the water of the pool. Then all was silent again.

Aaron scrabbled down his side of the draw and splashed into the water of the pool, having to swim a few strokes at the middle. He paused briefly when his feet touched bottom again to scoop a few mouthfuls of water that rinsed the taste of the long wait from tongue and throat. But water was not what he needed to slake his thirst. Quickly he was running out onto the other beach, shaking away excess water as exuberantly as a puppy splashing after a bath. He wiped his eyes with the back of his hand to clear his vision.

The eyes of the creature dulled completely as the man leaned over it and lifted the head. Aaron's hand felt into his wallet and brought forth a sharpened blade. He sawed at the jugular for a moment, then his mouth went to the sudden wound. He grimaced under the first acrid taste of blood, then drank his fill. It was more than a minute before he dropped the head and settled back on his haunches, wiping his mouth on his arm.

The little scurriers, irrepressibly curious, were already making their way back to the waterhole, although they stayed well clear of the interloper. Aaron watched them for a moment, then suddenly laughed out loud, a boisterous cry that rang out of the draw and was caught by a breeze which carried it out across the plain, where it was at last torn completely apart.

He stood then and hoisted his kill by the hindquarters until the mud of the beach ran gray-red with blood and there was only a slight trickle still coming from the wound. He dropped his burden then and yawned, stretching the tensions of the long wait from his body. His nostrils took in appreciative samples of the cooling night air while his eyes darted about in an apprehension no less constant than that felt by the creatures which had fled before his attack. Satisfied at last that no enemy had caught the scent of death, he settled beside his kill and began to enlarge the knife wound.

The man strained at his task for a moment and then the tough hide began to part. He worried at the opening, even to the point of bending to it and using his teeth to pull a tough piece of tissue taut against the knife edge. And then it was suddenly moving freely; soon he had severed the head and then the spinal cord was cut loose with three savage chops.

He held the head aloft for a moment, pleased with his prize and his success. It would make a fine trophy for the row of good-kill poles outside the Elder's house. But he was far from home—too far even to make practical the idea of caching the head for later retrieval. His journey had carried him this far only because the need for meat was so desperate in the village. It was with only slight regret that he swung the head around his own in a wild movement of both arms, then flung it into the brush along the shallow end of the draw. Almost before he returned his attention to his own task the little ones were burrowing into the meat and brains of the relic.

It was the work of less than an hour for Aaron to dress out his kill, after removing the skin entire. He hacked loose the choicest portions—he could not carry the entire carcass back home, but he left little for the carrion eaters beyond bone and gristle. Once the meat had been sewn into the skin, the flaps of skin that had been the legs pressed into duty as carrying straps, he plunged into the pool again for a swim that refreshed him from his labors. Before clambering out he drank his fill of the water, even to the point where his gut strained and his stomach bulged.

Then he came out of the water and kicked around in his path until he uncovered the stone that had killed his creature. He hefted it once, happy that it had not been lost, and slipped it into his wallet. He shouldered his crude pack, adjusted the straps until the weight felt comfortable against his shoulders, and worked his way around the pool and out the shallow end of the draw. Then, without a single look backward, he set out across the plain. He headed ever southward, feet moving in a deceptive loping run that rapidly covered the miles.

The cloudless sky was thick with stars, clustering in on each other so tightly that they lent a faint glow of their own to the planet below. In a few sectors the stars clustered so thickly that they made up nebulous masses, even strong-shaped clouds. The soft grass of the plain was colored a faint silvery hue by the starlight, while in the highlands dew sparkles winked back highlights of the star glory.

The night was filled with a sound all its own, easily discernible to the trained ear of the runner even over the faint hiss of his flat drawn breath and the tiny slap of his feet gliding over the ground. There was the constant susurrous of the insect world, unseen but ever busy, the faint cry of distant loneliness as a plains creature called for its mate, the sharp scream of victory as a night flyer found its prey. Even the very air made soft sighs as a gentle breeze touched the passage of the runner.

All sensations were duly recorded and ignored as being of no special interest to the man. Twice he shifted the burden of his kill, smoothly, without interrupting the steady ground-devouring pace he had set. The planet possessed no major moon to interrupt the unbroken succession of stars wheeling in their constant precession, although their beauty was blacked out once by the vast bulk of a stratosphere-trodding wind dreamer. Aaron noted the coming of the shadow by the sudden hush behind him. It overtook him, then moved slowly ahead. His heart beat faster for a moment as adrenalin plunged into his system. He feared the wind dreamer even though he realized that it could take no notice of his presence here. The shadow vanished ahead and he relaxed back into his normal pattern of quick breath timed to the rhythm of his legs.

The hours of the night passed with never a hesitation in the southward journey, as though he were instinctively drawn in the right direction. Dawn found the never-changing plain of the night giving way to a low, rolling series of foothills. Fifty miles further on, to the southwest, a massive mountain range loomed, thrusting forth peaks distinguishable even at this distance as separate entities. Their tops were universally lost in the haze of the upper atmosphere. Aaron's folk considered those mountains the birthing place of the storm and the clouds.

The range marched on toward the west, gradually losing shape but severing half a continent before it finally trickled out into a gradual slope that broadened into the great continental shelf. Just south of Aaron's position, however, the mountains stopped quickly, broken off by some ancient planet-shaping cataclysm. The runner automatically shifted the direction of his path to the eastward, a course that would take him through much of the hilly country, although the land was already deteriorating as it merged with the desert that he had been paralleling for the entire night.

Aaron continued on until the sun stood full above the horizon, then stopped at the crest of a low hill, shading his eyes against the stark glare. He peered southward. A mile further, an abortive attempt by nature to push the mountain range northward after eastern progress had been halted had left a jumbled configuration of naked rocks. Aaron recognized them and again broke into his loping run. Another twelve minutes brought him to the base of the rock pile.

The highest point of the several masses was perhaps a hundred feet higher than the immediate surrounding ground; just below the peak a ledge sprouted unexpectedly, half a dozen feet wide and extending perhaps thirty feet around the chimney shape of the peak. It offered remembered haven, and Aaron began to climb the rock face without hesitation, toes digging into the most minute crevices, hands grabbing at opportunities that hardly existed to gain purchase and height. A casual study might have considered the bare face of the chimney unscalable without tools, but within minutes Aaron was on the ledge.

The ledge had seen frequent use, as testamented by gnawed bones and bits of feather debris that showed where haven seekers had rested in the past. Aaron looked up to where a flat stone protruded from the face of the cliff a few feet higher than the ledge proper. It formed a natural shelf for his burden of meat, which would be slowly baked by the daytime sun. After stowing it carefully he took a last look around the countryside just traveled, and that still ahead. Seeing nothing of particular interest, he curled up in a slight depression just beneath the shelf, just long and deep enough to provide protection from the sun. Aaron was asleep within seconds.

The fading light of the afternoon brought him to full and immediate awareness of his surroundings. He lay still for a moment, eyes barely cracked far enough open to permit a survey of the ledge. Satisfied that he had received no unwelcome company during his sleep, he came to his feet in one lithe movement. He padded to the edge and looked down at the ground below, and was again satisfied when his search discovered nothing.

He stared for a moment toward the north, and the plain, then turned and clambered up the remaining face of the rock pile until he broached the crest and had an uninterrupted view of the land to the south. He stayed there for perhaps ten minutes, taking full advantage of the last of the afternoon light, then worked his way back down to the ledge. He brought down his pack; the meat now well cooked.

Producing his knife, he hacked off a fist-sized chunk and began to worry it with his teeth. It was tough, but he was used to that; his hunger was soon appeased. Then he worked into the center of the bundle and produced the largest piece, slicing into the center of it with his knife. Spreading the cut wide, he kneaded the edges of the meat until juices began to gather in the bottom, forced out of the flesh.

The juice slaked his thirst; he was still carrying a bellyful of the water from the waterhole, so there was no danger of dehydration. Which was just as well, considering that the worst part of his journey still lay ahead.

Darkness fell completely while he was finishing his brief meal, a totality mocked by the uncountable array of stars in the again-cloudless sky. Aaron stood up, relieved himself over the edge of the ledge, then shouldered his pack. He carefully retraced his steps downward, jumping the last eight feet, landing lightly on the balls of his feet and coming erect into the ground-devouring half run, half lope that quickly sent the miles piling up backward beneath his heels.

This rolling countryside was more sparsely populated than the plain. Now, for a short time, the vegetation turned a riper green, then began to grow lush. Aaron topped another of the low hills and stopped, gazing down at a swift-moving river. He turned to look up at the mountains; when he had last come this way, four days earlier, this stream had been little more than a brook.

Now it was a thunderer, born of waters come high from the mountains under the chance melting of snows just below the eternal winter line. The river headed across the continent, away from the mountains and skirting the north edge of the desert, reaching for the eastern sea impossibly far beyond the ken of the plains folk.

Crossing was obviously impossible at this point. Aaron immediately turned eastward, coming down off the hills and following the river's course until it broadened out in a good-sized low valley, widening in the space of little more than a mile from scarcely a hundred feet to almost ten times that. Its current slowed and softened in the valley, now nearly tamed and easily conquerable. A dozen miles downstream, however, the valley narrowed again and the pace quickened; the river would not know such placidity again for hundreds of miles.

Aaron picked his way along the bank of the stream until he came to a natural cove, offering harbor for an array of driftwood. He splashed into the water, still icy cold, and moved among the debris, considering and rejecting a number of pieces until at last he found one suitable to his purpose. It was a short log, half a dozen feet long and nearly a foot thick at its center, and only slightly water-logged.

He hooked his free arm around the log, moving the burden of his pack until it rested as much on the log as against his shoulders, then kicked his way out into the main stream of the river. The current plucked softly at him; he drifted with it for a while as it carried him in the general direction of the middle of the stream. But after a few minutes he realized that his progress was too slow; he started paddling against the current, aiming for the other shore—still nearly five hundred feet away.

The simple ark was awkward to control; it refused to go where he willed it. Aaron leaned his strength into it, trying to force the heavy log to obey—and suddenly he leaned too far and felt himself being carried forward, over the top of the log, pulled by the weight of the pack as it shifted away from him.

His motion was slow enough that it seemed only a matter of seconds before he would regain control—and then he was dashed face down into the water before he could take breath against the shock. Blinded by the night, he almost immediately spluttered for air and began to struggle. He lost his grip on the log and nearly lost the pack, which seemed determined to carry him straight to the bottom of the river.

And just then they did hit bottom, first pack and then man. It was not as far down as he had anticipated, for the pack had caught on a bar that in normal times was a grassy knoll overlooking the stream as it flowed fifty feet away. For a moment the pack held him against the knoll, and then he was struggling free of the imprisoning burden, kicking upward to the surface, the fingers of one hand still holding tenaciously to the one strap of the pack.

He broke surface just when it seemed that the fire in his lungs could no longer be controlled and that he must take in water to soothe the pain. The new air cut into him like a knife, doubling him over, but he still managed to keep his grip on the pack. He took in several more shallow breaths and trod water for a moment, then managed to bring the pack to the surface.

Aaron realized that he was being carried downstream with the current. Already it seemed to be quickening about him, and although he tried to strike out for the shore it remained stubbornly out of reach. And now the pack was becoming waterlogged.

He struggled against the pain in his chest and the growing numbness in his limbs. It would be so easy to give up the pack, but it was as though his body were refusing to allow the abandonment—either man and pack would come through together, or neither would survive. Still, the burden was almost lost to him more than once as his body was strained beyond its endurance and could no longer obey his commands. Man and bundle were swept down the stream for several miles as the current continued to quicken. He tried to swim against it, across it, but his struggles were useless. And now the noise of the river was growing ever louder as it once more entered the steep banks that changed it from placidity into an uncontrollable monster.

When his feet finally touched bottom Aaron was so exhausted that it was a minute and more before he recognized what had happened. The river had suddenly broadened into a much wider valley, the last cul-de-sac it would meet before the final plunge into a course of rapids that was hundreds of miles long, cut through a series of deep canyons that had never been penetrated by his kind. In the space of a thousand yards it widened nearly six times and grew so shallow that the pressure of the current almost disappeared. The shore was nearly a thousand feet away, but the water was so placid that it could be waded through with almost no effort.

He stood chest deep in the center of the river for several minutes while his senses adjusted to the sudden change. Slowly his senses began to function again, although at a much lower level. His night vision probed both shores and then he began to move—although his first steps were in the wrong direction. He corrected quickly and pushed his way out of the stream—pack still trailing as the strap was wrapped tightly around his fingers.

The water was still icy cold despite the change in its strength, but Aaron was so numbed that he ignored the chill. It took him nearly ten minutes to reach the shore and clamber out onto the grassy beach where he collapsed into an immediate sleep.

Half the night slipped by while he slept. Occasionally the helpless form of the man was investigated by bolder night prowlers, but none were strong enough to attack so large a creature. The god of fortune kept larger beasts of prey well away from him during his helplessness.

When he finally awoke his inner clock told him that long hours had passed. Aaron started to rise, then his battered and bruised muscles struck out at him and he dropped to the grass as though he had been felled. The red haze of pain kept him down until he could slowly bring his extremities under control. At last he sat up, carefully, and began to take stock of his situation.

His first thought was for the pack—then he relaxed slightly as he discovered it, then continued with an inventory of his own person, checking for cuts and violent damage. There seemed to be nothing more than bruises and contusions, all of them bearable.

Then he touched his wallet. It was empty.

Aaron rose quickly to his feet, ignoring the protest of muscle and nerve tissue. His night vision had returned, and he cast about anxiously to the edge of the river and for a space of five hundred feet along either side. But there was no sign of knife, sling, even rock. There had been a few other items in the wallet, of personal and talismanic nature, but the sling and then the knife were by far the most important of his possessions. Without them he was defenseless.

Aaron felt naked. He knelt beside the pack and permitted himself a moment of recrimination. Then he was up and reshouldering the pack. He moved back along the river bank, casting upstream for the trail he had been following earlier. He was surprised at the distance the river had carried him, for it took more than an hour for him to regain the trail. But he had no further thoughts of regret for the misfortune.

Although there was nothing to mark the trail apart from the surrounding countryside, he was soon following it as easily as if it were a highway. Again he was loping through the rolling countryside, which gradually grew more sparse with each additional mile from the river. The hours of the night were quickly consumed by the pace the runner set for himself.

At last, too close to dawn, Aaron came to the end of the low hill country. Stretching out before him was the north finger of the vast desert that he had been skirting for the past two nights. The arid waste cut clear across the heart of the continent, three thousand miles east and west and nearly a thousand miles from the southern reach to the northern, where its march was cut short by the continental mountain range.

Only this one extrusion of sand and wasteland had managed to force its way northward, around the unprotected eastern end of that barrier. The sand spread perhaps fifty miles ahead of where Aaron now stood, a waterless sea lapping greedily at the more blessed fertility of the north. Fifty miles across—and two hundred miles northward—the desert was the last obstacle to his reaching his village, which stood a few miles beyond the opposite side of the desert. The wasteland stood between Aaron and his home.

If it had not been for the unexpected encounter with the mountain-born river he would have reached this point early enough in the night for there to be a good chance for him to make the crossing before the sun stood high enough in the sky to strike him down. Now he was going to have to wait for another night.

He settled down on his haunches and studied the desert. This was familiar land to him, although he had crossed the waste stretch no more than a handful of times in the past. Still, he knew that there were places of haven out there, like the sea of which the desert was a dry mockery. There was one oasis perhaps fifteen miles out. It was scarcely more than a dripping of brackish water down the side of a boulder that had been cleft by an ancient spring, but it was enough to nourish a scattering of low brush—concealment from the extreme heat of the desert day. Such protection was necessary to any living creature caught by the daylight for, as harshly as the sun treated the plain, its burning of the wasteland was much crueler.

Fifteen miles—and there were perhaps two and a half

hours until dawn. At his normal pace Aaron could cover that distance with very little extra effort.

But he was near exhaustion. The battle of the river had taken a heavy toll. He tried to gauge the remaining hours of darkness by the position of a few of the brightest stars, but such a clock was at best unreliable. If he had not met the river his inner clock would have kept perfect reckoning, but he knew that even that could not be trusted in such a situation as this. He stood at the edge of the desert, hesitant, more cautious of moving out into this river of waste than he had been of moving into the river of water.

His sense probed the night and caught the faint, distant murmur of thunder. Faint flickerings about the peaks of the mountains showed where a storm was undergoing birth pangs. But he knew that the chances of a storm moving out over the desert were slight. On the rare occasions when one did, it usually dumped its water content quickly, while the parched ground as quickly devoured any traces of the moisture. The only true danger in a desert storm lay in being caught in low ground by a flash flood.

Aaron assessed the dangers of the storm and in a matter of seconds forgot about it. He was eager to move out, to try for the oasis—for it was fifteen miles nearer to home. He would reach the village that much earlier during the next night, and the thought was tantalizing almost beyond bearing.

But the knowledge of what it would mean to be caught on the desert by the day, without shelter—without protection—was sobering. A strong man whose tissues were bloated with water might last as much as four hours. A man in weakened condition might not live through the first hour.

Aaron did not try to fool himself; he knew that his condition was weaker than prudence dictated. Yet he was a gambler—a weakness that more than once had nearly caused him to be stricken from the rank of hunters. He believed in taking risks greater than the Elder could accept, and only the fact that in every case the risk had paid off to the benefit of the village had saved him in the past.

He considered his situation for a time that at most could be measured in minutes—and knew even before he assessed the risks completely in his mind what his decision would be.

Pack once again secured, he set out into the desert. . . .

CHAPTER TWO

Tomas was hungry.

This was not a situation of particular note, for the boy was frequently hungry. The citizen's ration had been designed to give minimum support to those who engaged in minimum activity—the law-obedient citizen who stayed where he belonged, in the safety and comfort of his own cubicle, occupying his time, as the Empress commanded, in watching the public networks. The true citizen had little need of excess calories. On those rare occasions when boredom penetrated to the core, there was always the dark red bottle of happiness to wash away the ennui in erotic sleep.

More than a million citizens followed this routine in Grid Center alone, while the great urban towers that dotted the countryside for a hundred miles around the Center were said to house a thousand times that number. Whether true or not, the figure was inconceivable—what difference between a hundred million and a billion when all were nothing more than ciphers in the consumption process that was slowly converting the resources of the planet into energy ash? The difference of a factor of ten was as nothing: a blink in the cosmic eye, as the universe measured time.

Whatever the total, the vast majority of the citizens were law-obedient, living as the Empress commanded and demanded. Still, in every large grouping the statistical probability of anomalies existed. There were those who were discontent, who were active. Tomas was such a one; he had been out of the junior bachelor's dormitory for hours now, moving through the shadowy subcity that underlay Grid Center. He had already missed the midday meal, which was why he was now hungry.

He carried rations against the possibility that this might be the night when he would be unable to return to the dormitory. The single slice of yeast loaf was little more than crumbs now, held in shape by the wrapping. A dozen times his hand had slipped inside his shirt to fondle the envelope, and more than once to half remove it, but each time the knowledge that it might be more needed later stopped him.

Even so, he could not prevent his stomach from grumbling loudly as he passed into one of the service corridors. He paused for a moment, slipping behind the bulk of a halted repair robot to make sure that no one had followed him from the public corridor.

This place was deserted except for an occasional robot trundling by on some mysterious errand of its own. None of them paid heed to the boy. Tomas followed the corridor for nearly a thousand yards, heart in his throat for fear that he would meet a human supervisor. He knew that he could not explain his presence here—dangerously close to the sublevels of the palace itself. But he reached his goal without incident. The key he had been given activated the access door to the electric service tunnel, as promised. A moment later he was through the manhole and descending the ladder into the maze of conduits and cross-cables.

This was the first time Tomas had been permitted to come this far and he stopped for a moment to look about in frightened fascination at the underlevel of the city.

Martin had said that these cables carried the main power supply for the entire city—everything except the palace and Grid Center itself; they were on separate self-contained nuclear energy power. The boy understood nothing of what he saw, though, and after a moment he stooped and crawled for perhaps a hundred yards beneath the largest of the conduits, until it suddenly bent to the left.

There was a space beyond the bend, perhaps six feet wide and three times that long. Martin was there, and two other men Tomas had never seen before—and another. His eyes went first to his friend, who smiled a greeting, and then were arrested by the fourth adult.

Mother of gods! The boy swallowed, not really believing that it was a lady of the palace. She was tall and stately—although not as tall nor as stately as the ladies appeared to be on the public broadcasts. A cool blonde, she was dressed in something scarlet that was nothing at all like a citizen's dress. At first Tomas could not tear his eyes from her face; and then his gaze moved down to the single bared breast. Never had he seen so private a sight —not in the crèche, not even in the junior bachelor dormitory, where the young men were considered old enough to be matched with the opposite sex.

"What's the boy doing here?" demanded one of the strangers, a surly blackbeard.

"We need a runner," said Martin. The tall man rubbed at the burn scar that crossed his left cheek and rose almost to the corner of his eye. "Tomas has performed well for me. I promised him a bit of unusual excitement this night."

"Foolish," said Blackbeard. "This is no place for kids."

"What better place?" asked Martin. "He has a stake in

the future—the future that we are trying to change for him. That is our code."

Blackbeard chopped his hand out in signal that he saw no purpose in continuing the discussion. At a sign from Martin, Tomas moved to a place in the corner and sat down. He was out of the way, but in a good position to see and hear everything that happened.

During the next twenty minutes three more men arrived, all strangers to the boy. The first two were surprised at the presence of the lady, but the third accepted her without a word. He seemed to be in command, for with his coming the others broke off their private conversations and gathered around.

"It's time for a bit of excitement again, gentlemen," he said after a glance at the lady. She smiled coolly and raised her hand and let it fall. The fabric of her dress floated down more slowly, catching Tomas's attention, but when he moved his eyes to look at her he could not help but stare at the pinkness that was her nipple. He flushed with embarrassment but no one else seemed to notice.

"We want to stir up the palace," he said. "No little gesture this time—no guards suddenly missing from the inner gardens. In the long run that only causes a little extra paperwork—the Empress can call up ten thousand replacements in an hour and a million in a week. The Empire runs on paper—we achieve nothing productive when we stuff a few more cubbyholes."

"What then?" said Blackbeard.

"It would be nice to stir up the citizens, wouldn't it?"

Blackbeard laughed. "Nothing will stir those cattle except for the proper slogans from the broadcast network. A citizen knows just two emotions—hunger, and loyalty to his Empress."

"True," said Martin. "And as yet we do not control the broadcasting."

"Which leaves hunger," said the leader.

Blackbeard grunted. "All right, don't keep it to yourselves forever. What's the fun for tonight?"

The leader smiled. "I think it will be something to satisfy even your yen for the dramatic—and bloodthirsty enough to perhaps scare some uncertain backbones all the way up to the First Level. We have four quarter-kilo nuclear devices. One for each of the main food-processing centers, and one for Old Town. If we are careful and don't get caught—in advance—we can destroy the food network for the central city."

"It will take months to replace the processing centers," said Martin.

"Replace?" It was one of the others. "Why? What's to prevent Grid Center from patching them back together? They can have things back to normal in thirty-six hours."

"The devices are dirty," said the leader.

An uneasy stir ran through the men and they turned to look at each other. Tomas listened in fascination although he did not understand a word that they were saying. The only reason he was here was the fact that Martin was his friend—and he would do anything for the man who had rescued him from the boredom of the dormitories and the ordained future of the home cubicles, once the Empress had chosen his mate for him.

The boy had wandered out of the dormitory on his own, for he was vaguely dissatisfied with that life, although he could in no way explain that dissatisfaction. He was seen, the first few times he left, by the dormitory supervisor. A black mark was entered against his record but nothing overt was done to stop his explorings, for many boys experienced just such urges during puberty.

Virtually all of them would settle down properly soon enough—as soon as they discovered that there was nothing more interesting in the portions of the city open to them than they could find on the networks.

Tomas did not return to the routine that he was expected to follow throughout his life, however—on his third journey outside, he met Martin.

It was not a chance occurrence. The man had spotted the boy earlier, but the opportunity to accost him did not arise. When it did, Martin lost no time in showing him the fascination of life below the culture of the city —a life that Tomas never could have discovered by himself. Soon the man had showed him how to circumvent the censors in the dormitory so that he could come and go almost as he pleased. And now, a dozen meetings later, he was being introduced to a way of life that no citizen could have imagined.

The question had never been put to him, but should the situation arise Tomas would gladly give up his life for the man.

Blackbeard was the first to break the silence that had descended after the leader's announcement. "How dirty?" he demanded. "What's the yield?"

"The bombs are powerful enough to render the food centers beyond repair," said Martin. "The force of the blast should be contained within the centers, for they are all protected by twenty-foot-thick reinforced concrete walls—proof against attack from the outside. They are not defended against attack from within, which is how we will take them. The contaminates have a half life of about ninety hours, which is enough to insure that the sites won't be approachable within a reasonable period. Yet they are soft enough to be contained by the existing walls."

"Once the centers are destroyed," said the leader, "the Empress will have to have food brought in from the urban towers. The effect will spread, for we are making a very large hole that will have to be filled quickly. I'm sure the palace does not want to face the possibility of a citizens' revolt."

He gestured with his right hand and Martin produced a document case. The leader opened it.

"We have false ID for the three of you who will carry the devices into the centers—you'll go in as replacements on the night inspection staff. The devices are all timed for 0745 hours, which should give you time to be well clear after the day shift takes over. We've managed to get a schedule of the inspector's duties—god knows there's little enough that can go wrong to make you really have to perform. Just be sure that the devices are well hidden, so that they aren't discovered before the time—or while you are still in the center."

"We choose by lot?" asked Blackbeard.

"As always." The leader nodded and looked to the lady. "Lady Dianne, would you do the honors?"

The lady still had not spoken, but now she came forward to accept from each man a slip of paper with his name. The leader added his and then looked at Martin.

"I choose not to be in this draw," said Tomas's friend.

"Oh?" The boy thought that the leader seemed disappointed.

"I cannot draw," he explained. "I am already committed. I choose Old Town for myself."

"Um." The leader looked at the others, but there were no protests. "Very well, you have chosen. M'lady, will you please draw the first of the remaining three targets?"

It was Blackbeard; he seemed satisfied. The other targets went to two of the other men whose names Tomas had not been given. All three accepted their false identity tokens and a change of costume from Martin. They changed quickly, heedless of the presence of the woman, and when they were done they bore the appearance of midclass workers.

Tomas was familiar with the idea of sabotage from the thrillers that were always popular on the public networks. But the idea of sabotage striking so close to home was something entirely new—the fictional violence was always set in the distant past, or on some far colony star. Still, the intent of what was happening had finally penetrated his level of understanding and he was excited.

He was disappointed by the bombs themselves, however. Rather than looking sinister, they were nothing more than flat packages, no larger than the yeast-loaf envelope that he still carried in his shirt. And they quickly disappeared, giving no sign that the three chosen were armed with anything deadly far beyond the possibility of personal defense.

The men began to leave as they had come. After twenty minutes only Martin, the man Tomas thought of as the leader, and the lady were left to share the place with the boy. The man looked at Tomas carefully.

"Are you sure that you know what you are doing?" he asked.

"I'm sure," said Martin, softly.

"He is only a boy—and completely inexperienced."

"Tomas is loyal," said Martin. "As for experience, no one is experienced in what we will be doing tonight."

"I'm sure that you are right," said the lady. "After all, it is your own life that you are risking—is it not?" It was the first time that she had spoken, and Tomas shivered deliciously as the musical notes rang clear—not at all like the harsh voices of the midclass women workers he had known in the crèche, or the giggling nonsense of the girls he had so far met in his own class.

"It is my life, m'lady," said Martin deferentially. "I ask no one to take a risk that I will not take for myself."

"A noble statement." She nodded. "As for myself, whenever I find myself feeling noble, that is the time I most mistrust my own motives. Captain, it is time to leave. Will you be so kind as to escort me back to the palace."

"M'lady." The leader inclined his head and followed her out. Tomas could not help but be fascinated by the fact that she did not lose her dignity even when stooping to crawl under the conduit.

The boy was alone then with his friend. Questions crowded at his tongue but he restrained them, waiting for Martin to speak. The man busied himself for a moment in clearing up the meeting place, removing a trace of debris, stowing it and the document case in some place that the boy could not see. He had left out his own bomb; now he picked it up, examining it carefully for a moment. He looked at the boy.

"Not much, is it, Tomas?"

"No, sir."

"Yet it has a great capacity for mischief—and perhaps for good. Have you ever been to Old Town?"

The boy shook his head. "Is there really an Old Town? Ma Crichton used to say that it was just a bogey story, to frighten bad children."

"Oh, it's real enough," said Martin. "And it's a blight bad enough to scourge even the bogey man. But with a bit of luck you may see this as Old Town's last night."

"Are you going to bomb it?"

"If I can," said the man. He stared off at something that Tomas could not see. "If I can . . ."

He seemed to reach a decision and suddenly ducked

under the passage, moving so fast that the boy was hard put to keep up with him. They went out a different way from the one in which Tomas had entered, and it seemed that they were in the maze of underground passages far longer. When they finally surfaced and came out into the service passageway, Tomas was lost.

There was nothing familiar about the public corridors beyond, either—although there was a much heavier concentration of human traffic here. And well mixed with the midclass and the citizens were the powder-blue uniforms of the palace Guard. Strangest of all to the boy, however, was the large percentage of adults—men and women both—that he could not place by class.

The pair brought casual scrutiny from many of the passersby, but little more than that; there were others of his own age about, and not a few of them were in the company of older men. After Tomas grew used to the people around them he recognized that the city itself was strange. There were few residential quarters here, and most of those seemed to be on the midclass level—once he even saw a barracks of the Guard.

Martin knew where they were even if the boy did not, and he was heading for some destination, paying little attention to his satellite. It was not until they suddenly reached a small park that the man stopped and turned around, as though looking for the boy.

"Old Town, Tomas."

"Here?" The boy looked about in amazement. Martin smiled, and led the way into the park and through the other side. Suddenly they were moving between two of the vast pillar supports—and for the first time in his life Tomas was not under the protection of the city.

He looked up at the high sky, but Martin was disappointed when he did not react. It was not Tomas's fault

—he did not know how to react. After a moment the man touched him on the shoulder and indicated their goal.

Old Town had once been a part of the city's suburbs, some hundreds of years before. When the old city center was torn down and rebuilt Old Town was prosperous suburbs, the proper place for the upperclass to live. But, as always, in time the centers of affluence shifted to the high levels of the new city and Old Town gradually became a slum. The new city grew away from it, until now Old Town was a festering sore on the southeastern border, a place of perhaps ten thousand crumbling houses and no city services at all.

Despite the lack of services Old Town was brightly lighted—for the denizens had little love of the dark except when it served to shield their own activities. They had rigged every possible form of portable power, until now a myriad colors blazed from every block and a cacophony of impossible sounds rose like an almost visible miasma.

The place Martin had chosen as his entrance to Old Town was guarded by a bar gate which was in turn watched by a vicious character—and upon seeing him Tomas realized why he had not been able to place the strangers he had seen. His costume was archaic, although the boy could not know that. He carried a long, wicked-looking truncheon, which was tipped with a six-inch blade, and he raised the weapon at their approach.

"Business?" he said.

"Our own," said Martin. "It's none of yours."

"You want to go through my gate," he rasped.

Martin laughed. "Solomon's gate, you mean. Stand aside, ugly one. I'll pay a fair toll and not a bit more. Two silvers for myself and the boy."

"Six," the other demanded.

Tomas did not see the motion, but suddenly Martin

was holding the truncheon, the blade tickling the throat of the ugly guard, who was backed against his own bar.

"Two silvers," said Martin, softly. "I am an honest man. I have no need to cheat Solomon out of what is rightly his. But when I speak to him again, I will be sure to mention the guard who thinks he can charge triple, so that he may pocket half."

The guard's face whitened and he shook his head. "All right—you win!"

Martin lowered the truncheon and handed the silver across cheerfully. The guard rubbed his throat and held out his hand.

"My strong arm," he said.

"I think not—I'll leave it at the bottom of the stairs."

The man stared at him murderously but made no further protest; he raised the bar and permitted them to pass. Once through the portal Tomas discovered that they were on what had once been a broad promenade, but the tiled floor was now broken and overgrown with weeds. They were in near darkness here, looking down at the blaze of Old Town. The promenade's own lighting had been destroyed long ago.

Martin hesitated only long enough to be sure that the guard was not following them, then he led the way to a broad staircase that seemed to curve down into darkness. It was farther down than the boy had earlier realized; it was a good half hour before they finally reached the bottom, and he was feeling the unaccustomed exercise in the muscles of his thighs.

A broad esplanade ran straight from the bottom of the stairs into the heart of the old suburb. Once it had been tree-lined, but most of them were long gone, leaving only stumps. The street was lined with litter but the path before them was still clear well beyond the first group of houses, which began a thousand feet away. Although

several of the houses were contributing to the mixture of
bright lighting, the street seemed to be deserted. The man
surveyed it carefully and then began to skirt around the
entire section, keeping to the shadows, ever alert.

Tomas followed him, and soon the boy became aware
that they were being watched. There were men out there
in the darkness—several times he was sure that if he had
reached out and touched a darker shadow, it would
come to life. But there was no move to interrupt them,
even though Martin had abandoned the truncheon at the
foot of the stairs as he had promised. Tomas was sure
that it would not be there to be retrieved by the guard
when he came down.

They seemed to be circling the entire development,
following an ancient road that curved in a gentle manner;
Martin kept well within the shadows and soon the bright
center of Old Town was behind them. The boy could see
that it stretched much farther than he had originally
thought. At last the man stopped and held out his hand
to the boy, drawing him up close. Tomas moved to him,
then saw that the man was pointing into the darkness.
After a moment he saw a soft glow of well-concealed
light.

Martin moved forward, the boy at his heels, making his
cautious way to the house of the light. He stopped again
and watched for nearly five minutes, but Tomas saw
nothing at all. Then they were moving to the rear of the
house, crossing a baked-clay lawn that seemed to be
crowded with piles of debris. Yet the man moved through
it surely, never disturbing a single stack.

Reaching the house was almost anticlimax. He touched
the ancient doorbell and a moment later the door
opened on silent oiled hinges, although there had been
no sound of the bell ringing. All was blackness inside
until the door closed behind them. Then soft light sprang

into being in the corridor, showing a massive man who seemed to be bouncing up and down before them on short, bowed legs. He was naked to the waist, and the rolls of fat cascaded down from his breasts. On one of them was tattooed a bright red rose, the nipple seeming to peek through shyly; the other sported the tattoo of a leering eye.

"You took long enough."

"The business could not be hurried," said Martin.

The man shrugged and turned to lead them into the front room. The rooms that stood open off the corridor seemed to be piled high with stuff impossible for the boy's mind to catalog. He was fascinated by the riches that surrounded him, for there had been no taste of them in his lifetime. Tomas could not know that what appeared to be riches was really nothing more than garish junk.

The house must have been larger than it seemed from outside, for the front room was very large indeed, sporting a dozen massive chairs and half that many sofas. Most of them were overflowing with pillows, but Martin cleared one of the sofas and sank down on it with a sigh. The fat man took the largest chair of all, which was still none too large for his bulk.

"Well, do they have a chance?" demanded the fat man.

"Arrghh!" Martin spat toward a silver spittoon. "How could they? The bloody fools—playing at revolution! It seems so simple to tear down the structure of government. It should be simple, considering the rotten nature of the government that we have. But many good men have been taken by the palace Guard because they mistook that nature—too many of our men. Our best men. If only we had some of them with us now."

"We don't," the other man said with a grunt. "Did you bring back the toy?"

Martin reached into his shirt and produced the bomb, tossing it over. "A pretty toy. Pretty enough to fool the few technicians the underground can muster now."

"And expensive," said the fat man.

"I hope the Guard is easy on them," said Martin.

"Oh, they'll be transported, sure enough. The mind wipe is still an efficient weapon—how can your enemy harm you when he no longer knows that he is your enemy?"

The boy stared at them in turn, not understanding. He thought that Martin had introduced him into a revolutionary cell—but now it seemed as though his friend were betraying those they had met earlier. He ached with questions to ask but could not find the words with which to ask them. After a time, however, he drew the attention of the fat man.

"Are you sure it was wise to bring the boy?"

"Tomas is the hope of the future," said Martin, and in the glance he gave the boy was a certain pride. "We have to get them young, train them properly."

The fat man shrugged. "I think it's a mistake—but it's your mistake. He's baggage, at a time when we cannot afford—"

His words were cut off by a sudden explosion at the front door, and then it was thrown violently inward. There was a shocking blast of light that burned a brilliant afterimage across the boy's retinas, but in that same instant he received the impression of figures rushing into the room. They were goggled against the light bomb and held hand weapons.

And then he was blind. But he could not mistake the sound of men moving toward him. He reached out his hand, trying to find Martin, and pressed forward. His arms went around someone and he was struggling with one of the invaders.

"Tomas!" It was Martin calling to him, but he seemed very far away. The boy had to strain to hear him and could not spare the effort from his struggles. He beat out wildly, only a few of his blows striking home at all, none of them with telling effect.

And then he found the man's gun. Instantly both hands went around it, trying to pull it free from the other's grasp even though he could not see it. He heard the harsh breathing of the man.

"Tomas! No—stop it, boy!"

What was Martin saying? telling him to do? Little matter; he found the trigger plate of the gun and was bending all of his strength against it, trying to force it out of the man's grasp. Suddenly there was another explosion of almost-visible light, and the man seemed to relax, no longer struggling.

Tomas tried to stand up, but there was a strange numbness in his chest. He put up his hand but could feel nothing—nothing at all. The only sensation was that of cold. He was aware that Martin was again calling his name, over and over, and this time there seemed to be tears accompanying the man's voice.

"Tomas! No, boy, no!"

Martin's arms went around him; he recognized the man's grasp. "It's all right boy. Nothing is going to happen, Tomas!"

He heard the words but he did not understand them. Suddenly he could no longer feel any part of his body—even the thoughts seemed to be evaporating from his brain. He tried to raise his hand but he was not sure that he accomplished the gesture; he tried to speak Martin's name. Martin was his friend. He would do anything for his friend.

Even die . . .

CHAPTER THREE

The night passed quickly for Aaron—too quickly; dawn was tinging the eastern edge of the sky before he was halfway to the oasis. The pink band across the horizon was warning to the night creatures that it was time to seek shelter; the day would last for nearly seventeen hours before they would be able to venture out once more into the cool and quiet of the evening.

He quickened his pace, ignoring the protest of his strained muscles, but the oasis was still a good thirty minutes ahead when he stopped suddenly, wheeling southward. His nostrils flared broadly, mouth drawn back in a teeth-baring grimace. His hearing probed outward, picking up the now-constant sound of thunder, no longer a murmur. It had been reinforced, and at some unknown recent moment had crossed the line into distinct audibility.

He looked to the mountains but the sound was not coming from there; that earlier storm had ended. But now the smell of airborne dust was in the air, choking and clogging his throat, making it hard to draw a comfortable breath. He could feel the thunder now, impossibly, through the soles of his feet. It was a vibration that whipped the ground, not the atmosphere. Under the faint blush of the onrushing day he could see the dust already in the air. A vast cloud of it seemed to be rolling up from the south, filling the horizon from end to end and towering high against the sky.

Fear started his heart pounding, the glands again pouring adrenalin into his bloodstream. Only one feared thing could cause such a dust cloud:

Lopal!

Following an evolutionary pattern similar to the cat races that seemed to appear on every hominid-habitable planet yet discovered, the lopal was the most feared predator on the continent. On other planets the cat was a lonely creature, choosing always a life apart from its fellows, content with its solitary heritage. On this world, however, the pack instinct had replaced that of the individual hunter.

Nothing stood before the lopal packs. The size of a full-grown man, a lopal could bring down animals several times its own size. When a pack hunted through a valley little remained behind but bones, scraps of hide, and trampled vegetation.

The great packs had been hunting the southern half of the continent for the past dozen years, but now they were on the move northward again. They killed indiscriminately, from joy as well as necessity; after a period of time the land could no longer support even a small pack. Hunting had grown difficult in the south, the game thinned out to the point where it would take years to replenish the former level.

And at some unknown time, months past, a single pack probed farther south than ever before, even into the cold of winter. The pack was seeking new sources of good hunting, easy food, but it was to meet with disappointment. It reached the snow line and recoiled, then retreated northward.

Weeks later the pack met up with another and joined

its cousins. The language of the beasts passed on the message that the easy hunts were over. The packs joined others, moving ever northward as they picked up more and more recruits—until now more than ninety percent of the lopals of the south were making the great run for the once-again easier lands of the north.

The great desert served as the primary boundary of their hunting territory, but now they moved out across it, ignoring the waste and the terrible heat of the sun, one joint gigantic venture numbering more than a million individuals. They stripped the land of everything edible in their vast hunger; the border country five hundred miles to the south of the desert was as barren now as the desert proper. Some of that land would never recover from the passage of the beasts, and the desert would extend itself a few more miles with every migration.

They moved across the great desert, their hunger growing with each passing mile that saw no game, no food. No stop was made for rest. The great packs thundered on into the north, where they would begin a reign of terror unseen since the last shift had sent the great migration moving into the south.

Lopal! The name was enough to strike terror into the hearts of adult and child alike . . . even though few of Aaron's people had ever seen one of the beasts. Those who had seen kept the stories alive. Nothing could stand against them.

And the great pack was pounding down the final finger of the desert, heading straight for Aaron.

He wasted only seconds in recognizing the menace and no time at all in reacting. It was too far to retrace his steps; his only hope lay with the oasis, scant protection though it would afford. Terror lent extra strength to his muscles and the pace of his flight steadily increased until the thirty minutes was cut by a third. The sun was already well above the horizon when he spotted the small cluster of vegetation that marked the boundaries of the oasis, but everything was obscured by the still-rising cloud of dust.

A pile of rocks occupied the center of the oasis, the tallest rising perhaps sixty feet above the floor. There was easy access to it—easy for any predator as well as for the man. But there was no other place for Aaron; he vaulted to the topmost surface and dropped flat against it. After a moment he realized that he was still carrying the pack; he shrugged out of it and used it to pillow his head.

Already he was feeling a terrible headache. Now he lay flat on his face, eyes closed tightly, arms cradling him against the side of the pack to offer a slight filter to his breathing. Feeling completely helpless, he waited for the main body of the migration to reach his sanctuary. The cloud of dust grew until it was a blinding, choking screen that cut off all impression beyond that of being alone in the universe.

The noise grew impossibly louder, until it seemed as though he were in the center of a vast, hollow drum—a drum that was being played slowly, with great effect. The pounding passed beyond the point of hearing; he was deafened. He placed the heels of his hands over his ears, trying to keep out the sound, but it poured upward, reaching through the substance of the rock and into every nerve and fiber of his body.

But the attack of beast that he had been expecting did not come, and gradually Aaron came to the realization that there were no bodies rushing past below. Loud though the sound of passage seemed to be, the pack was actually miles away. His run for the oasis had actually carried him closer to danger. After a time he moved, trying to peer through the choking clouds of dust. The dust quickly settled over the few parts of his body that hadn't been exposed before, caking to the sweat streaks, filling his hair and matting it wildly, filling his nostrils until it seemed that it was no longer possible to draw a single life-giving breath.

He lay down again to ease the pain of breathing and lost track of passing time. There was no day and no night under the dust. He soon became aware of only the sensation of aching that had settled into every part of his body —into his chest from the dust he could not avoid breathing, into his bones and nerves from the vibrations of the great passage that came through the rock.

The sun reached an unnoted zenith and started to slip back down into evening before the rear echelon of the pack finally thundered on past, into the north. Aaron lay still for another hour, breast heaving with agony, before he became aware that it was over. He could hear nothing but a shrill ringing, and the dust in the sky would hang on for days before finally dissipating under the desert winds, but the great passage was over, for this sector, for another dozen years. It would be months yet before the great pack dissolved into the least of its components, though.

Aaron rose to his knees then and managed to stand. It was some time before he dared the descent, dragging the pack along with him as much for a cushion against the fall as from a habit that had made the bundle a part of himself. He reached the crevice from which the small spring normally spouted.

It was completely choked now with the dust. He dug into the stuff, pulling it away until at last he found a bit of mud, and then kept on digging until he had cleared the water's path. He buried his face against the small trickle, letting it wash over his face and carry away the surface accumulation of dust, then rinsed his red-rimmed eyes. At last he swallowed a mouthful, ignoring his body's protest. He took another mouthful, rinsed it around and spat it out, then once more forced a small amount into his stomach.

He sat up then and thought about food, but his teeth ached at the very thought of eating. He rested for perhaps half an hour in that spot, occasionally letting the water fall across his fingers, and then he stood and cast about for shelter against the remainder of the day—although the sun had made no progress in its attempt to break up the dust cloud.

A sudden noise stopped him in his tracks, half poised on the ball of one foot. He glanced about, apprehension starting his heart to pounding faster.

The sound came again, a low rumble.

It was felt, not heard. Aaron turned cautiously and saw the great beast a hundred yards away. It was surveying him, great yellow eyes slits against the still-hanging dust cloud, mouth gaping and drooling, saliva slobbering around needle-sharp teeth that were nearly fangs.

Lopal!

He moved backward slowly until his back was against the rock facing. He reached for his waist, for his sling—and remembered that it was gone. There was nothing.

He edged along the rock, still holding on to the pack, when his foot came down on something hard. He looked down and saw that there was a fair-sized stone—several stones. The lopal was watching him, not moving any closer, as it considered something outside of its previous experience. The man slowly squatted and picked up the large stone. It fit well into his hand, balanced either for throwing or for use as a hammer.

Then another shadowy form was moving out of the dust, coming to a stop near the first. Then a third.

The three beasts watched him. Their ribs stood out clearly against slack black hide, their store of energy burned away under the nonstop migration. There had been little food along the way, and their months-old hunger had become a force that would drive them on against any odds.

An eternity seemed to pass in a few seconds. Aaron's tongue licked over his parched lips, thickened until it almost choked him. His right foot slowly drew back as though trying to find purchase against the boulder. But there was no safety to be found there, even if he managed to scramble back up to the top of the rocks. At best it might gain him a respite of seconds.

The beasts watched him, not moving. They were outriders from the main pack, straggling behind in the vain hope that something edible might have been overlooked by the vanguard of the migration. It had been far too long since their efforts had been rewarded; even the urge to continue the northward journey could not overcome the powerful need of their hunger.

They began to circle in.

Aaron moved back along the rock facing. The lopals separated now, coming in at him from three sides. He reached down and loosened the straps on the pack, moving slowly lest they decided to rush him. When he straightened again a generous chunk of meat was in his right hand.

Suddenly he screamed and whipped the chunk of meat around his head to build up momentum. Then he threw it straight at the middle of the three creatures.

The lopals had been caught off guard by his scream of defiance. One reared back for a second, then realized that the prize was food. The beast to Aaron's right watched him for a moment, then suddenly darted in on its companion, trying to grab away the piece of meat. They began squabbling, rolling about in the dirt.

The third creature ignored them, never taking its eyes off the man. Aaron licked his lips again and hefted the rock, conscious that it was a pitiful weapon against such a powerful opponent. He tensed, and saw that the beast did the same, drawing taut, powerful muscles as it made ready for the leap. He waited until the lopal was committed to its move, then brought up his stone and let fly. Even as it left his fingers he was diving away to the left.

The rock caught the creature in the left eye. It screamed with agony as blood spurted forth, blinding it. Claw-extended paws struck the face of the rock and scrabbled for a hold; it slid to the ground in a heap, thrashing around, trying to find the hated man. Again it screamed, momentarily drawing the attention of its companions. But their hunger made them lose interest. They returned to fighting over the bit of meat.

Aaron drew back a safe distance from the wounded lopal, watching it worsen its situation through its blind thrashing. It was striking out at the air, trying to find the man. He moved cautiously around until he was against the rock, then started to sidle between the rock and the beast. He waited until it was facing the other direction, then drew in his breath and scooped up another of the rocks.

In the same motion he leaped upon the lopal's back, arm whipping tight around its neck, heels digging into that scant area where hind legs joined the body and the beast's claws could not reach him to rake at him. He began to pound at the ridge over the good eye.

The lopal twisted, trying to reach him with its teeth,

and one fang did touch close to an ear. But the man was as powerful in his own way as the beast. He pounded repeatedly at the eye ridge while his other arm tried to choke off the beast's breath, never loosening his hold. At last his efforts paid off as the skull smashed.

He dropped the rock then and tried to force his fingers down into the cavity, but the threshing of the lopal grew so wild that he was thrown off and nearly twenty feet away—and fortunately well away from the other pair. The maddened creature ran straight for the rock facing, pounded heavily into it, then dropped, stunned.

For this one the battle was over. It lay in the dust, sides heaving for breath as blood poured out of its head wounds. After a minute the heart was no longer able to sustain the struggle, for there was no energy in the system for it to draw upon. Suddenly the labored breathing stopped completely.

Aaron drew breath into his own aching lungs, then struggled back to his feet just in time to see the argument between the other two settled. One was still stronger; it cuffed the other away and dragged the prize out of the clearing.

The other resented the loss. The man had been forgotten in their squabbling, but now it turned its attention to him. It growled a warning as the man moved cautiously to put the dead cat between himself and the new attacker. He found another of the stones and picked it up for a weapon.

The lopal moved toward him, but then, as Aaron had hoped, was distracted by its dead companion. It circled the body warily, smelling death, considering the possibility of turning this into food. It was weak enough to know that there was little profit in attacking something that clearly could fight back when there was already dead meat available.

Aaron did not give it the opportunity of making a final decision. When its back was to him he ran in, screaming again. A leap put him on the animal's back, feet digging into the underbelly, arm wrapped around the throat while the other hand pounded the stone against the bony ridges.

The beast was too exhausted to fight him off; it screamed and tried to rear but the bones shattered first. Aaron hooked his fingers into the eye sockets, digging through the mashed bone and flesh and gouging out the eyes. Then he was probing farther, his fingers jabbing into the brain.

The lopal paused for a moment, all action arrested. Its throat started to form a scream of anguish but before it could be uttered the body went slack; it collapsed, dumping the man into the dirt.

Two were dead, one still alive. That one finished the piece of meat and perhaps gained a little strength from the nourishment. It stared at the man, seeming to realize that here was something totally outside of its experience. The lopal was supreme on this planet; other creatures were not supposed to fight back—nor even to attack. And should insanity force them into such a rash action, it was incomprehensible that they should win.

A bestial intelligence burned within the huge yellow eyes. It considered the man before it: naked, helpless, apparently easy prey. But two of its brothers were dead. It rose to its paws, hackles raising the short hair on its back. A low snarl of defiance burst from its lips.

Aaron regained his rock, hefted it. Barely a dozen paces separated them. The lopal moved forward as the man tensed himself for the attack, right foot sliding back a few inches. Beast and man screamed together: beast and rock passed through the air together. A sudden twist of the animal's head, however, threw the stone off target. It bounced off the hide behind the eye as the lopal landed on top of the man.

Instinctively Aaron wrapped his arms and his legs about the body of the beast, burying his face against the hide between the front legs. The position prevented the lopal from bringing its teeth into play but did not stop it from bringing up a claw that raked down the man's back.

Aaron screamed. His feet lost their grip as the beast reared up again, rising to its full height and leaving him dangling by his arms.

Then one foot drove upward, between the lopal's hind legs, finding the natural bulge that protected the genitals. The beast screamed now as the hardened toes found their target and dug in. Pain drove all other thought from its mind as it plunged wildly, trying to shake loose its tormentor. But Aaron only clung the harder.

Once again the foot drove in, finding its vulnerable target. The lopal reared again and lost its balance, falling heavily on its side. Every vein and artery bulged against its skin as the animal's heart worked mightily—and Aaron suddenly buried his teeth against the jugular. Blood spurted as the vein was ripped apart. The lopal gave one last cry before going into its death throes.

Aaron rode with it until the body finally shivered into quiescence, then slowly relinquished his hold. He stood up. Forgotten were the aches that had seemed to have robbed his strength; now he felt only an extreme weariness. He took a single step and staggered, then dropped to his knee. Yet there were things he had to do; he would not yet surrender to his body's needs.

He stood again, dragging breath deep into his lungs,

then made his way to the water supply. He could not take much into his stomach but it was a relief to again let it rinse over his face.

Satisfied, he found one of the stones and used it as a hammer to pound the teeth from the dead lopals. The pack was where he had dropped it, most of the burden of meat still safe. He bundled up the bloody teeth with the meat.

The afternoon was nearly gone; the haze caused by the dust cloud was slowly deepening into a blood-reddish hue. There was still more than thirty miles of the desert to be crossed and it could not be done during the day. But Aaron did not possess strength enough to go even a mile.

He rinsed his mouth one last time at the water trickle, then found a resting spot beneath low brush. Sleep quickly overtook him. . . .

CHAPTER FOUR

The night was muggy away from the controlled environment of the city, the heat pressing down from above and pushing against the tall towers, reaching up even to the imperial apartments in the palace. Even there, where a public reception filled one of the great courts and spilled over to a score of more private rooms on levels below and above the acknowledged festivities, the feeling of oppressiveness was almost electric. It was enough to drive the Empress Karyn from her guests, even though the palace was controlled to the point of absolute comfort for her.

Ducas Martin found her on a balcony that could be reached only from a small sitting room that was open to no more than a dozen men in the world. She was leaning on her elbows in a manner undignified for the royal presence, watching the play of colored waters in the great fountains that began fifty feet below; she was trying to trace a single explosion of scarlet before it vanished into mist on the half-mile drop to the gardens. She seemed not to hear the soft warning chime as Martin entered, and he waved away the liveried servant before formal announcement could be made, moving up behind her. But before he could reach out she spoke without looking around.

"How did it go, Ducas?"

"Badly, m'lady."

Karyn straightened then but did not turn to face him for another moment. Apart from the fountains below that lit up the palace tower, the city was dark, silent, a vaguely seen bulk in the moonless night. Only to the south was there anything to disturb the serenity of the night, where a blast of garish colors marked the presence of Old Town. Except for that excrescence, they could have been alone in a city of the dead, for there escaped to them no sounds of the revels which hosted within. More than dead, the city could have been empty of citizens, the subjects and wards of the Imperium all locked safely away behind windowless walls where they would not intrude on the peace of the royal presence. This time and this place were the Empress's favorites and she hated to give up this part of herself as she turned to Martin.

"Did you fail?"

Karyn was all in black tonight, complete to wig; the only contrast in color came from the pearls at her neck and the stark cameo that served to gather revealing fabric over her breasts. Her face seemed empty of makeup, her lips bloodless. Only her eyes took perverse life, sparkling with the blackness of her accoutrements. She was in her late thirties, a year or so younger than Martin; but so long as she was Empress the arts of the royal cosmeticians would keep her eternally young.

Martin waved a hand. "Near enough to failure—Stennock's hounds came bursting in like comic opera flatfeet. They nearly destroyed everything—and took Solomon. I had barely an instant's warning to save my sight." He did not mention the greater loss that still numbed him.

"Stennock is a fool!" Her words were flat, stabbing. "I should have demanded him declassed years ago."

"You would not have won," said Martin. "Even then he was powerful—and now he is the Council. The others do not understand their domination. They're so used to accepting advice from him that it's too late to change them. We can only get rid of them—if Stennock will permit us to do so."

He turned to pick up a crystalline globe that had been free-formed by being heated nearly to incandescence and then plunged into a bath of liquid helium, but only his tactile senses played across it. His eyes never seemed to leave the face of his ruler.

"Is the game lost, Ducas?"

He shrugged. He had changed clothes, and with the upperclass gauds came a transformation that would have permitted no more than one or two of the men in the tunnel to recognize him as he was now—even the boy Tomas could have looked straight into his eyes and never seen his friend. His features were somehow softer, almost puffy, dissolute. Only the hard glare in his eyes signaled the presence of the other personality within the shell of this man. He set the globe down on a sideboard and without invitation poured liquor into a warming glass. He turned back to Karyn, the bell-shaped glass held between both palms, all ten fingers extended as he slowly rotated the vessel.

"The game is never lost, m'lady, so long as we have a player to field against the opposition—and so long as the final bell has not sounded. There is still time. But I cannot say how much is left. The situation has degenerated to the point where victory may no longer be possible."

He sipped at his glass, studying her over the rim as he gave the released fragrance time to penetrate the olfactories. The liquor had been warmed now to his body temperature, but it slid down his throat as though it were icy cold. The burden of alcohol seemed to explode through his veins, the cold heating him so that beads of sweat formed on his face. There was a singing sensation in his ears, and every sense seemed heightened. He was strongly aware of the presence of the woman, and the tip of his tongue wet his lip. He touched his face with a wisp of linen.

"What now, then?"

"It may not be too late—the first thing is to recover Solomon before Stennock can order the mind wipe. If indeed the wipe is not a standing order."

"It would be so much easier if I were Empress in truth, not just in name!"

The frustration was ancient; the powers held carefully away for ten generations now, since Karyn's many-times-great grandfather had wrested control of the Supremacy from the dying democracies. The byword of empire was "reign, not rule," a simple postulate to the continuance of the royal tradition. It had been borrowed from an ancient nation of this very planet, where it had worked well. In supposition, the royal person was always free to make demands and to win whatever cause sponsored. But the actual power lay in the Council of Royal Advisors, at present a dozen men and women, and the Council suffered the Empress only on occasions of state, or whenever it seemed politic to use her tradition as a buffer between themselves and the people they ruled in her name. The Advisors might be hated as individuals and as the Council, but the populace was reverent to the position of the Empress.

"You are a goddess, Karyn," said Martin now. "The gods are above the mundane problems of rule. Your people love you above themselves, and would sacrifice themselves to you at an instant's command."

"A foolish waste."

"Agreed. However, your position does offer you protection even as you conspire against your own government, never forget that."

"Would you sacrifice yourself to me, Ducas?"

He closed his eyes a moment. Then, "Some might say that I have done just that, Karyn. I serve you when I might better serve myself. Even now, what might I not win if I concentrated my entire will—even to the Council itself."

Karyn laughed, a musical note that stabbed mercilessly into his soul. "You forget yourself, Ducas—you forget who you are."

"I am what you have made me," he said, suddenly cool.

"Yes, indeed you are that. I thought that you had forgotten how I rescued you." She reached out then and let her crooked finger trace the line of his jaw. Suddenly his hand was around her wrist, bending her back as he moved closer to her. The liquor he had drunk paled beside the intoxication of his senses as he bent to kiss her. For a moment she was his captive, and then she was breaking away, fingers turned into claws that raked across his cheek.

"Damn you!" She breathed heavily and brushed her lip with the back of her hand. "You go too far, Ducas!"

"It's you who reminded me of my base origins," he said. "I act only as my Empress wishes."

She laughed again. "Perhaps so. Ah, to be young again, Ducas! To be as we were when I picked you from those gawking bandylegs to be my escort, and then to be my own aide. Remember how shocked they were?"

He did remember, and wished that she had not brought back those memories—for with them came always the constant reminder that, unlike those others of his Karyn-appointed class, he was no one. He did not know the name of his mother or the profession of his father, for he was born unwanted into a crèche and raised in the children's barracks. Only the potentialities tests given to all children had marked him for other than the eternally controlled existence of a citizen, sent him at the age of six to the schools that would eventually graduate him into the Navy. His education was limited to those subjects which prepared him for service to the Imperium and no other, for which he was always grateful to the figure of the Emperor. He did not realize that he had traded one cell in the honeycomb of life for another that was no larger in scope.

It was chance and no more that had saved him, brought him into the real life of the Empire. The Princess Karyn had been visiting the Academy on some now-forgotten occasion of state, probably to honor some now-dead winner of a battle out on the fringes of the Empire. In honor of her visit the Academy had prepared a ball—but forgot to inform her in time to permit an escort. In a fit of pique she spotted Martin, an honor cadet, in the foreranks, and chose him to be her companion for the evening. The Academy superiors were so properly shocked at her evasion of protocol that she had determined to continue the game, demanding the appointment of the young man as her naval aide. An amused Emperor acquiesced to this inconsequential demand of his child, and thereby changed the entire future of that once-youth.

Martin tried to remember himself as he had been then, but could not; the past was gone, that unthinking automaton completely alien to the man he had become. Even his name had changed, for the harsh gutturals befitting a citizen had been an aural intrusion upon cultured patterns. He had not even thought of that name in nearly twenty years; and now as he formed the two simple syllables in his mind he could not relate them to the person that he had been.

There were times when he wondered what life might have been had he not been selected out by the tests, had Karyn not chosen him from the rank of cadets. He could no longer imagine the stultifying existence of the citizen, most of whom left their warren homes only to be fed and bathed, and the latter only on direct command of the Empress. Would he have been one of the discontented, the potential rebels, slipping at night from his barracks like Tomas? Or would he have accepted everything that was done to him, demanded of him, his potential atrophied to nothing.

Ah, such speculation was idle, useless. The past was, and could never be changed. The future was all that was worth worrying about, for that could be changed by men determined to proceed against all obstacles. And he was determined.

But Karyn . . . what of her dedication? Was she in this incipient rebellion only because it offered possible amusement to jaded appetites? Although he had known her intimately for twenty years now in every sense except the physical, he knew that he had never penetrated her inner thoughts. She was smiling at him at this minute, but was she pleased? Or still angry because of the liberty he had taken?

He knew then that he wanted her, completely. And he hated her for never having chosen him as lover. He could ignore the reality that a lover had never lasted more than six months in her favor, whereas he had been with her his entire adult life. He had served her a hundred times in ways that she would not want made public—did he not have the right to demand now that she serve him?

"Ducas, you are upset." Had she read his thoughts? She

reached out to touch the mark she had made on his face. "Does the struggle for freedom become too heavy a burden?"

"Freedom," he said then. "What will it mean, Karyn? Have you given full thought to what will happen if we succeed? It is your throne that will be lost."

"But the throne is a curse on the people," she said. "I do not wish to be the owner of an empire of slaves. I would gladly surrender the throne if the Empire would crumble away at the same time. But we know that it would not, Ducas."

"The Empire may be too heavy to fall," he said. "It may be too early for our rebellion."

She shrugged. "Then such it will be. Even the ruler of all men cannot control the Fates, Ducas. But we must try, must we not?"

"Yes." He sighed. "We must try."

"Take me out to the party, Ducas. We must join our people, lest they mark the insult."

He nodded, but turned to the sideboard and poured himself another drink before joining her. As he held the glass between his hands he looked down to her portrait in the place of honor over a mantel. It had been painted as she was when he had first known her, for she had succeeded to the throne barely a year later. And physically there seemed no difference between the image and the reality. Always slightly larger than life-size, the woman in the painting seemed touched by something godly, an easy object for the citizens to venerate, even to worship. Her hair, in truth the color of fire, in the portrait was piled high, caught in place by a single jeweled comb, while the dress was a deep wine velvet unlike any fashion seen away from the throne. He could recognize that woman but at the same time the physical Karyn seemed almost a stranger. And how was he to know which was the reality?

Then a strange emotion passed over him, surprising him, making him turn to study her as he drained his glass. For a moment he could not give it name . . . and then he knew that what he felt was pity.

And that made him bold. "Karyn, have you never known love?"

She seemed astonished and it was a moment before she answered. "I think so . . . once. There was a man who affected me as no other man ever has."

"What happened?"

"He was transported."

It was his turn to be surprised. "A rebel?"

"So it was said. I never believed it, for I was certain that I knew his heart. And he never spoke of rebel thoughts to me. He was a friend, that I know, both of my father and of me."

"What happened?"

"One day he disappeared. Several months later I was told that he had confessed to complicity in a plot against my father's throne."

"His name?" The questions hurt deeply, but he could no more not ask them than he could force himself to stop drawing breath.

"Aaron Caldwell."

At first the name meant nothing to him . . . and then it signaled familiarity. It was a name from the distant past, from the time before he had become Ducas Martin, but it was important enough to force its way through the overlying decades of trivia and important subjects blended together. That early Martin had been little concerned with events outside his tight world and so the fact that he knew Caldwell's name meant that he had been important.

"But he was of the Council!"

"He would have been," said Karyn. "Aaron was my father's closest friend, most trusted advisor."

"They must have thought him extremely dangerous, to strike so close to the throne. Why didn't your father act?"

"My father died then—Aaron was the one who brought me the news. He did everything for me then, until he disappeared. I tried to find him but it was months before I was told what had happened. And by then it was too late—he was already transported."

"You didn't try to find out more?"

"I was young then, Ducas. I knew my limitations, for the Council had someone by me always to point them out. I did not know my powers, my abilities. If it happened now, I could do something, but then . . . if it were possible to turn back the clock that is where I would will the hands to stop."

It was always too late, they said. . . .

A private elevator brought them from the royal apartments almost into the heart of the party, discharging them into a hidden alcove. It was late—it was past midnight when Martin had arrived at the palace—but the party was just moving into full tension. There were several ballrooms occupied, as well as a number of rooms for more private entertainments, and all seemed well packed with pressing, sweating, frantic upperclassmen. Yet within minutes every guest seemed to know that the Empress had arrived, and they began to form around her, eddying quickly into a whirlpool of laughing, talking, calling faces. In less than a moment Martin was separated from her and spun out along the fringes of the crowd to find himself instantly alone, ignored by the mass of people who considered themselves honored to be in the presence of the Empress.

But he was not alone for long, for even as he watched with envy those who reached out to the woman a man bulked out of the darker shadows along the wall and came to him.

"Ah, Martin." The name came awkwardly to those used to titles that instantly marked the position of the bearer in the scheme of things. But Martin owned no title except his name, for his position was perhaps unique in the palace. And there were those who would have protested the awarding of any appellation not earned by birth.

"Lord Stennock." He nodded brusquely, not hiding his dislike for the man. But the Prefect of Police pretended not to notice the expression of contempt, though it was well for him that he was not a sensitive.

"I understand that you were accidentally caught up in one of our ventures into Old Town."

"Is that what you call it? I was lucky to escape with my sight."

"Some of my people are zealous in the discharge of their duties." Stennock was easily the largest man in the crowd, and broad enough for two men. But although he was not fat there was the impression of softness to his bulk, as though it were inflated with air rather than substance. His scalp was shaved and painted silver in current fashion, the fire gem on his cheekbone immense of the kind but seeming lost there. "Of course," he added, "if a man happens to be in a place that is of its nature apt to be of special interest to the guardians of the public morality, then he should accept the consequences of his being there. No?"

"I have every right to be in Old Town," said Martin. "I can go anyplace that I wish."

"Within reason," agreed the other. "Always within reason. There are such things as should be secret. And of course there are always the unlawful, which certainly should be avoided by the discreet."

"Old Town is free sanctuary."

"Even so, the guardians cannot be expected to ignore subversion as it grows. We don't mind the petty criminal —let them kill off each other and save us the expense. But we must at all times protect the Empire."

"You know my position," said Martin, deciding to speak frankly. "I was on the Empress's business."

"What business could the lady Karyn have with such as outlaws?"

"I cannot answer for her. You are free to direct your questions to her, however. But I must know what happened to the man called Solomon."

"He is in good hands."

"Release him."

Stennock's laugh was little more than a snort of derision. "We've waited too long to get this fish, Martin. I think we will keep him."

"I speak for the Empress."

"Perhaps so. But the Empress is not in a position to command her Council."

"If I have her command you directly . . . ?"

He shrugged. "Who can say what would come of the breaking of precedent? If I were to guess, I would think that it would not be as you wish, Ducas Martin. It might be best not to raise such a troublesome issue." He rubbed his nose then and let his finger brush across the cheek stone. "Of course, if the lady were to explain the reason for her interference with normal police duties . . ."

"The Empress does not have to explain herself."

"What a pretty thought! Of course, we know that the

truth is otherwise. It is the Council that does not have to explain to the throne. It is our place as advisors to tell the Empress what must be done. It is her place to acquiesce to our advice."

"As ruler, the Empress is supreme."

"The Supremacy is three generations dead," said Stennock. "It was given a merciful burial long after the time was proper. Nowadays the Council controls all power. Perhaps even the royal favorites are not beyond our reach."

What had Caldwell done to expose himself to them?

But Caldwell was twenty years transported. It was Solomon that Martin needed now, and he would have to activate the most private channel to reach him. But there was one more matter to raise with the Prefect.

"There was a boy picked up in the raid . . ."

"A boy?" His eyes narrowed in surprise. "Ah, yes, there was a barracks brat. Does he belong to you?"

"What happened to him?"

"I don't concern myself with children—"

"I must know!" he demanded. "Is he dead?"

"Ah!" He chuckled in knowing mirth. "I'll find out for you. You needn't fear—we wouldn't bother to transport a mere boy. And I'm sure that his mind holds nothing to demand the wipe—if indeed it is worth giving the wipe."

He produced a pocket communicator and spoke into it. There was a delay as the man on duty sought to track down the unexpected request, and then the Prefect was concentrating to hear over the bedlam of the party. Then he looked back to Martin and shrugged.

"The boy is alive, in police hospital. If you wish to see him . . ." Martin nodded. "I'll order a pass left for you at the main desk."

"Thank you, m'lord," he said, bowing stiffly. "Please forgive me, but I must leave."

"Oh, I understand, I understand." He grinned. "In your place I might hurry too. But may I ask a favor for a favor?"

"Sir?"

"Tell me what you were doing at Solomon's den."

"Indulging myself, m'lord. As is the right of all who serve the Empire."

Booming laughter followed him as he pushed through the crowd. . . .

CHAPTER FIVE

Dawn was coral haze to the east, wiped across with streaks of silver-gray as the layers of dust eddied through the air currents. The sun was swollen beyond recognition when it first edged over the distant mountains just as the hunter came walking toward it out of the desert. The vegetation had been growing steadily more lush as it fed off underground waters, and now he was among tall grasses and soon stunted trees that within the space of scarcely a mile towered twice as tall as the man.

There was barely strength enough for Aaron to put one plodding foot before the other, but he had never surrendered the burden of his pack. Now he found a remembered path and soon came to a familiar grove that sheltered a pond which was fed by a chill spring. He dropped to all fours by the water and buried his face in it, letting the water soak into the caked dust as a bit trickled over his teeth, making them ache with its chilled goodness. Then he was rolling into the pond, falling down through the water, letting it take him where it would. He did not feel the ache in his lungs as they grew short of oxygen, the red haze seeming a familiar companion rather than a warning. But one foot touched bottom, and his body drifted upward again, his face breaking through the water before he tried to breathe in liquid.

The sun was nearly an hour over the edge of the desert by the time he crawled out of the water, pausing to shake himself like an animal. Then he was finding the strength that let him stand erect, rubbing his eyes until the dotted circles moved from his vision.

There was no part of his body that did not in some way pain him. But he was alert. And now he was back in familiar territory, often covered. He purged himself with the pond water, forcing it down and then up again, and then drank sparingly, gathering up his trophies. Then he was back on the trail, heading toward a now-near goal.

Soon he was in forest, moving through tall conifers, the filtered sunlight a strange dappled color that created false shadows within real ones. And he was moving through silence, with no sound of creature to break around him; the woods might have been empty of every life but his own. Even the birds were gone from the trees, which were beginning to change in form as the land started to rise upward to a plateau of open meadows. Then he was standing on the rim of a lake-filled valley, and then moving down at an ever-faster pace to the village of tents on its north shore.

Aaron was seen before he was off the ridge, and by the time he reached the outer edge of the circle of tents most of the people were there waiting for him . . . waiting eagerly. Joseph the Elder was being led from his tent by a young hunter, leaning into his staff as he tried to see through eyes nearly sightless. Surrounded, Aaron threw down his pack and let out a wild cry of triumph. Then he was being embraced on all sides.

"Aaron?"

"Yes, Father," he said, answering the Elder's query instantly. "I am back."

"The news? Were you successful?"

"The news is bad—and good. There was no sign of the other tribe Rob reported. But the hunting is good. There is more game there than we ever saw in our best days."

"Then the curse has not struck everywhere."

"I saw no signs of sickness among the game. But I did see more!" he added, unable to restrain himself further. He bent and opened the pack and took out two of the largest teeth, then placed them in Joseph's hand, closing his fingers over them.

"What are these?" The old man felt them over, pressing the ball of his thumb against the fang. "What animal owned these, Aaron?"

"Lopal!"

The word exploded from him, and then more words came pouring out as he forgot restraint, telling of the great herd and of his battle with the three strays. Forgotten were his weariness and body aches as he danced with the sheer joy of telling his story. And his listeners shared his excitement, making jabbing motions with elbows and fists as he painted the scene. He finished by gathering up the rest of the teeth booty and tossing them into the air to be caught eagerly by the men and the women alike, afraid that they would miss out on a share in his performance. Even the half-dozen children of the village, the oldest barely beyond crawling, knew that they were hearing of a great marvel.

But at last he ran out of story to tell, having repeated himself three times over, and his voice was telling with the strain of breathing dust for the past day. He ran down then and placed his hand over the old man's.

"These two are the biggest and the best, Father—they are for you."

But the Elder was shaking his head, turning his hand palm up. He seemed to be staring straight into Aaron's eyes as he pressed the teeth back upon him.

"This is an evil thing, Aaron! The curse that has stolen

the game away from the forest and the valleys is as nothing to this. If the lopal have come back, then men must
leave. The two cannot exist together. There is nothing else
for it."

"But the lopal are not here!" Aaron's protest made him
choke. "They have gone north, beyond the desert. There
are none to bother us here—or on the far side of the desert. We are safe."

"When the herd stops running, breaks up, then they
will be back. By the end of the season they will be here
again." Again he shook his head. "I smelled them coming," said the old man. "I did not know what it was, but
I knew that it meant evil. The gods who brought us have
laid a double curse on this land. They can only mean for
us to leave."

"That is as I said!"

"We must go farther than you dreamed of, Aaron—we
must go south, to the lands that the lopal have abandoned. I have seen the great beasts, watched them when
the herds last made the great journey across the world.
Of those who came with me only I am still alive to tell
you of their evil. I tell you that men cannot stand against
them."

"We can!" said Aaron defiantly. "I have!"

"You were lucky," said Joseph. "The three you killed
were hungry, exhausted. The pack stripped the land of
everything, leaving nothing for its own trail. You could
not stand against one well fed."

"One man, no. But two men, three—yes! Together we
can stand against even the lopal. Together we will stand
against them, Father!"

The old man trembled, nearly fell; two of the nearest
hurried to help him to a seated position on the ground.
His eyes closed for a moment, his head tilted as though

he were hearing something beyond the hearing of the villagers. But after a moment he reopened his unseeing eyes and pointed his hand at Aaron.

"You issue a hunter's challenge, which is a good and a brave thing. But it is not a wise thing. You have not seen the lopal as I have—you have not seen a single beast rage through a village, destroying every tent and all those people who were not fleet enough to run into the forest. One beast—a dozen men dead!"

"Did they stand against it?" asked Aaron. "Or did they tremble and run, each man acting only for himself?"

"They did not try to stand against it," the old man admitted. "They could not. I tell you that you must leave this accursed land completely, Aaron."

"We cannot go south," he said. "No one has ever seen the end of the desert. That way lies only certain death. Would you have us go east, against the sun? Our swiftest hunters have followed it for a ten-days' journey, and everywhere they report that the curse has fallen over the land. There is no food to be won in that direction, not even for a single man—how can the entire village live there? I tell you, Joseph my father, that we have no choice but to cross the desert to where the game is still plentiful. We have no choice! If we stay here we face certain death by starvation. If we go where there is no lopal and no food, then the same thing will certainly happen. We must cross the desert!"

"Perhaps the gods intend that we should die here."

The old man spoke softly, so that only Aaron and one or two of those closest heard his words clearly. But Aaron rejected the words with a sudden chop of his hand.

"If the gods intended our death then why bring us here at all? Certainly the gods do not need the help of the lopal in so easy a task. They could kill us at any of the times that they have willed us to sleep."

"I don't know," said Joseph. "I do not have the answer for you. I no longer know what course to follow. I think that I am ready to die."

"But I am not!" said Aaron heatedly. "Why talk of death? Life is near to hand, begging to be grasped. The entire village can cross the desert in no more than three days—four at the limit. We can carry enough water for all, enough food for the children and the weak. Once across, then there will be a hunt such as we have never held in our greatest dreams! Our bellies will be full, so full that we will all grow fat."

"You do not have to die with me," said Joseph. "I am ready to make the journey alone."

The shock of his words moved Aaron back a step, hands held out palms downward as though to ward off the meaning of Joseph's words. He looked at the others, the thirty adults of the village. Seven of them were women, five of them gravid and one of the others recently delivered—for the women had come late to the tribe. There were many among the men who could remember the long years without the women, the years that now seemed empty beyond belief. But the gods had blessed them after a time, until now they were growing even without the aid of new sendings. Indeed, it had been more than a double handful of seasons now, two of the planet's years and during which almost all of the children had been born, since the last arrival from the land of the gods.

"I wish that I could see," said the old man, moving his head slowly from side to side. After a moment the tears grew in the corners of his eyes. "Without eyes I no longer have the power to understand what is best for the people. It may be that my day has passed, that it is time for me to make room for another. This may be the gods' way of telling me that it is time to stop living."

"The gods could not be so cruel," said Aaron.

"Who knows what motivates the gods? We know enough of them to know only that we know nothing of them. You said that you brought meat, Aaron? Good. I shall prepare my waiting feast, and then I shall finally know the answers to all questions. I shall meet the gods and know what manner of men they be, who can lay sleep over the whole world so that no one can see them in their actions. Perhaps they will take me up with them, to become a god myself."

"Father, Father . . ."

Aaron was not alone in expressing his grief, for he was joined by every one of the adults. They were openly crying, although they did not dare lament over that which their Elder had chosen for himself.

"You do not know what you are saying," said Aaron. "You have many seasons left before you. We, your children, need you. You cannot leave us, abandon us at this our most perilous time of need. Come, stay with us, grow with us! Let us care for you in thanks for the way that you have cared for us for all these many years."

But the old man was past listening to their entreaties. He rocked silently, clutching his staff to his breast, staring straight ahead at nothing and refusing to look toward their voices.

"I need the meat," he said. "I would prepare the feast for myself if I could, but my eyes have failed me. In this I need your help. Prepare the meat and bring it to me so that I may prepare my vigil."

———◆———

And so the Elder Joseph, appointed father of his village by the unknown gods who rule in the heavens as they rule on the world, shared his last feast with those who had made him what he now was. Five days passed after the feast of waiting, and during that time neither food nor water passed his lips. He sat ever wakeful before his tent, attended always by several of his people who had come to spend an hour or two where he would know of their presence. But they were not waiting for the gods and they could not stay with him for long. They could only hope that the gods would consider it enough that they never left him alone to meet the unknown, without a friend to help him should he slip on the way into death.

Aaron came often during the first days, sitting with him and talking to him. Occasionally the old man would respond to his questions by nod or gesture, although never with a word. But by the third day he was too weak to do even that much anymore, and on the fourth day Aaron came to sit with him for the final vigil, holding his hand to let him know of his presence, prepared to stay so long as the spirit should inhabit his body.

As he sat with Joseph he watched the activity about them as the others prepared to abandon that which was the only home that most of them had ever known. The men would come to the waiting pair whenever they encountered a problem that they could not solve of their own surety, addressing their questions to the older. But it was Aaron who gave the needed answers, and in such a way they decided to take no more than three of the tents, which would serve as shelters from the fierce desert sun. It was also decided that each would be limited to the utensils that he or she could carry unencumbered. Only the hunters were to carry all of their possessions, for they would be the ones to bear the burden of feeding the village even after they were finally relocated. The women and the three cripples carried only their seeds for the farming that would stretch the game in the new home; implements could be fashioned when they were safe in the new land.

On the morning of the fifth day the old man died. The moment of death came quietly, unrecognized by those who then surrounded him. It was several minutes before Aaron realized that the fingers were no longer gripping his. Joseph's eyes were open, and in the instant of death it was as though the cloud had been lifted away from them, leaving them clear to show him the way into eternity. And there was the trace of a smile on his lips, as though he had welcomed his death gladly.

The time of mourning must be brief, for they had already stayed beyond the time of wise departure, using some of their precious store of grain. Only the knowledge that game would be plentiful once they were across the desert let them decide against the strictest frugality, for with full bellies they would be stronger to face the arduous trip.

There was much still to be done and too little time to properly do it. The woman and cripples collapsed the Elder's tent, carrying the frame and the wrappings to a nearby high hill. There they constructed a bed for him, larger than he had ever needed in life, to show that he was fit to be welcomed among his equals, the gods. His prized possessions were brought then, and Aaron followed by himself, carrying the feather-light body. It was as though the weight had left as his soul had fled.

Everything that Joseph had prized in life was arranged around him as they prepared him for his eternal rest, eyes open so that he could see the sky and welcome the gods when they appeared. For perhaps ten minutes the people stood ranked down the hill, doing and saying nothing; then at an unseen signal they turned and began to drift back to the village, leaving Aaron to be the last, their duty to the old man finally done.

———————◆———————

By the time the sun was an hour in the sky the next morning the villagers were ready for the move. During the night certain of Joseph's possessions which were of value to the entire village had reappeared, distributed among several of the living, and no notice was taken of those who carried those items. They gathered together for a moment, looking back on that which they would never know again, and then the hunter Rob was pushing through the press of the crowd, bringing Joseph's staff to Aaron.

"This is not for me," he protested.

"You are the Eldest, Father," said Rob. "You have been here the longest."

It was true; Aaron had been here longer than any of those around him, even though several of the men seemed to be older in actual age. But there were none to question his assumption of the Elder's position. He took the staff as though he were fearful of handling it, but the polished wood fitted his hand well. Once, twice, a third time he struck it against the ground, and it was as though it had always been a part of him.

He turned toward Joseph's hill and held out the staff as though in thanks. Then he turned back to his people, to the ones who he must hereafter serve. They would follow him to whatever new land he ordered, until in time he became as old as Joseph. And that day would come, he well knew. Death was the one messenger who could not be refused.

There was a certain amount of sorrow as the villagers made ready to leave much of their wealth behind. The village had been a good one, Joseph wise in his decisions.

The lake had fed them, watered them, the hills surrounding them in comfort during the mild late season. In the early days there had been game enough for everyone; it was only in the past few seasons, since the coming of the children, that it had become necessary to seek wider for their food, to plant the fields with crops, even to send the unoccupied woman and oldsters out to gather natural edibles.

The land was empty now despite the thick grasses that covered the hillsides, the thick forests that had once sheltered the game. Even the berries, the nuts, were no longer abundant, as each year for the past three years the bounty of the land had grown less.

Three years . . . It occurred to Aaron, and not for the first time, that the span of time since the arrival of the first woman fitted within that number of days. And there had been a reckless one or so to claim that the coming of the women and the children was responsible for all of the recent troubles. But Joseph had refused to permit such talk, for only he could remember back to a time when the women had been here before. The gods had cursed the tribe by letting those first women die, and now he was certain that the long years of loneliness had been repentance enough.

For himself, Aaron could not see how the new arrivals could have affected the game, for they were brought by the gods. If they displeased the gods by being here, why had they then been allowed to appear? He had talked of such matters to Joseph, but it was the Elder's decision to allow no speculation on the subject, lest the conundrums posed be of ill nature.

"Wind dreamer!"

Aaron was startled out of his revery as the warning cry came from one of the hunters. Seconds later the shadow slipped over them, seeming to chill the air by its presence. The villagers were struck still with their fear, looking up toward the beast, and even Aaron felt cold around his heart. He had seen the creatures, always from a distance and out on the plains, but never so close to the village. Why had it come at this moment? He feared that it was an omen sent by the gods.

The great bird was circling, not moving off, and now it began to lower itself groundward, tiny jets of steam appearing around its wings as it released heated air from its bladders into the chilled upper atmosphere. The villagers were panicking now, certain that the beast was coming straight for them; several dropped their burdens and fled toward the still-standing abandoned tents or to the nearest woods. Most stayed in place, however, waiting for whatever fate the gods had decreed.

The beast was no more than a thousand feet above them now and Aaron could see that it was not by several measures as large as the legends and even his own distant sightings had made it. Still, it was a good size bigger than a man, and now he could see the great pinions that could knock a running man into death, the grasping claws that were strong enough to carry off any one of them. It must be looking for them. There was no way that it could not see the cluster of humans as it dropped still lower, the beat of the great wings felt now in the stirring of the air currents.

More of the villagers broke out of their frozen stance, panicked into running in whatever direction the position of their feet aimed them at the moment of flight. Only Aaron held to his position, frightened though he was, conscious that he was now the leader of the village in every way. He could not show fright before those who relied upon his courage and wisdom. And he was armed, for his slings and favorite stones were in his wallet.

He began to draw them out even though he was certain that a stone could do nothing to the great beast but annoy it into a direct attack. But he hesitated with the sling in his fingers. The wind dreamer still had given no sign that it knew the people were there, and he began to hope that perhaps it did not care. Whatever had brought the mighty bird to this rarely traveled section, it could not be hunger. He began to think that the beast would overlook them, going about its mysterious errand in its own time and manner.

The wind dreamer was no more than three hundred feet over him now, the great eye red, the pinfeathers beneath the wings a strangely beautiful pink. It gave no sign that it knew that the village and the humans were on the same planet as it soared over the tops of the trees, so low that twice Aaron was sure that it must crash into them. Then it regained altitude as it circled out over the lake, then came back over the village site. Suddenly there was a change in wing movement, and it began to climb higher into the sky, now moving away from the village and the lake. Soon it was gone over a line of hills and from sight.

Aaron suddenly felt weak, sitting down where he had stood, sweat suddenly pouring out of every pore. He leaned forward against the staff, closing his eyes as he offered a silent prayer of thanks to the gods. After a few minutes the villagers began to drift from their hiding places, aware that their chosen Elder was the only one of them not to have run from the beast. Rob and the other hunters were shamefaced, and there was a heightened respect for Aaron that showed in the way they could not look at him straight, held back from approaching him too closely.

"What did it want?" asked Rob.

"Only the gods know," Aaron replied. "They sent the great bird, and they withdrew it. It must be an omen; the message will be revealed in its time."

Wordlessly, without being told, the others began to pick up the abandoned utensils and possessions, ready once more to follow him to the promised new home. Aaron hesitated only a moment longer, reluctant at the last to abandon that which was familiar. The people had formed before him, a ragtail caravan that bulked in unusual places. He drew a single deep breath, struck the ground once with the staff, and led them out.

For himself, he knew now that he was not just taking the people to a new home. The world had changed from that which they had known so long, and he himself had changed most of all—he had met the harshest challenge the gods could throw against men; he had overcome the lopal. And now he knew that even the wind dreamer was not necessarily to be feared. As he set out on still another challenge to his gods he carried a new awareness of himself, and of what men could do and be. . . .

CHAPTER SIX

It was cold in the hospital, the chill cutting through layers of human fat to strike directly at the marrow, pressing against the spine, generating shivers that could not be warmed away no matter how thick the layers of protective clothing. Those who worked in the chill wore electrically heated coveralls but still the cold penetrated their defenses, as though it attacked the mind rather than the feelings.

An orderly was assigned to guide Martin down through the levels of impersonal and totally silent wards, giant filing cases of flesh without life, most of them given over to cold sleep as the simplest and most economic therapy for the treatment of large numbers of unimportant citizens.

Conscious that the orderly could not keep her eyes to the front, Martin was glad that he had not stopped to change before leaving the palace. Upperclass visitors were so rare here as to be without precedent in her experience. She was obviously impressed by his gauds and he noted with grim humor that she was taking every possible way to show him that she was available, should he be as the upperclass were usually pictured on the citizens' entertainment channels—kind to their inferiors, always willing to offer the properly humble petitioner their aid, and frequently willing to dally with the attractive female. It was the dream of many citizens and even midclass workers that they would someday be rescued from their tedium by the interference of the godly uppers. But the girl was not really disappointed when he failed to respond; indeed, success would have frightened her, perhaps into a panic that could only embarrass them both.

Tomas's cold cell was one in a long bank, ranked three high for the convenience of those who must care for him, buried lockerlike in the wall. The gleaming metal case was pristine, as though polished, but the ever-present chill of the atmosphere made Martin feel that to touch the casing would be to draw blemishes in an ultrapure rime. The orderly activated the view panel so that he could recognize the blue-cold features of the boy within, then dialed the chart, which meant nothing to him.

"Explain it," he said.

She studied the read-out for a moment longer than necessary, indulgent of the mysteries to which she was privy and this lord not. "Primary indications are that there is complete paralysis of the motor functions. Secondary postulates suggest that there is suspected destruction of the retinas—"

"Suspected?"

"The boy was brought here in stasis," she explained, "already in paralysis. The information given in the guardian report stated that he was directly exposed to both an actinic bomb and a moderate-force stun beam. In such instances there is almost one-hundred-percent probability that there has been irreparable damage."

"What is being done for him?"

"Standard procedure, m'lord, is to immediately place the patient in cold sleep, to give the body a chance to recover from the effects of the various tranquilizing forces. Otherwise there is apt to be erratic recovery, creating an impossible demand on the heart, the motor system."

The orderly was not young, but she knew that she was

not unattractive. Still, Martin's hard gaze embarrassed her, made her feel as though she had been caught out in some shameful wrong. She ran down, helplessly.

"Are all of your patients in paralysis?" he said then.

"A good many of them, m'lord. Most of those here were caught up in some civil disturbance."

"But is it necessary to dump them into cold sleep, every last one of them?"

"This is police hospital, m'lord," she said defensively.

"I'll wager the guard receives different treatment," he said. "What will be done for the boy?"

She was upset by his attack on hospital procedure, as though she were responsible for creating the standard. She was sorry now that she had ever tried to flirt with this cold man.

"Sufficient time will be allowed for recovery from the stun beam," she said. "Then he will be brought out of stasis and given a complete neural probe. If there is irreparable damage, if as suspected he is functionally blind, then he will be transferred to a determination center."

"Determination center?" The term was new to him. "What is that? Who makes the determination?"

"I don't know," she said, embarrassed again. "My work is limited to aiding the patients while they are here. Once they recover from cold sleep I don't see them again."

"But you have some idea of what happens there," he insisted. "What happened to similar cases in the past?"

"That would depend on a number of factors, m'lord," she said when he would not be put off, "hardly any of which I would have knowledge about. Considering the background of the case, I would suppose a recommendation would be entered for termination."

"Termination, eh?" He grinned, a humorless grimace that chilled her even more. "A beautiful word—determination centers for the termination of uncomfortable situations." She realized the mistake she had made in not pretending ignorance of everything that happened elsewhere in the system, in not sending this upperclass snoop to someone higher in authority at his first question. No longer was she attracted to him, either by position or by physical presence. He had somehow brought her to babble of the subject that normally was forbidden even among the other workers in the hospital. Certainly she had never revealed to a citizen or midclass worker the end result of hospitalization here.

"I wonder," he said, "do they dispose of them in the historical tradition, out of hand? No, I don't suppose they would be brutal—there is no reason for brutality in our golden age. It must all be done in proper manner, proper taste. I wonder when the killers were released from their dungeons—and by whom?"

"M'lord?" The words had come flat from his lips, seemingly without emotion. But there was a hard fire in his eyes that for this moment made her wish that she had never been selected from the barracks to assume this statused position in life. Better by far that she remained a citizen for all of her days. Still, she tried to defend the indefensible.

"The boy is only a citizen, m'lord. He is still assigned to a barracks, he has only a C classification as labor potential. I'm sure you know that only a fraction of A-potentials are ever chosen to serve. I've never heard of a C—"

"Get me a physician," he said, cutting her off. "Quickly. Someone in a position of authority."

She did have the presence of mind to direct the call around the normal levels of response, bucking it straight to the hospital supervisor. That person was no more used to visitors of such high place than the orderly, and thus

the unexpected may have been enough to forgive his failure to process the demand through normal procedures and
thereby through the ranks of the Prefecture of Police. Instead, he hastened to do as Martin bid.

Twenty minutes later the demanded doctor arrived, ir-
ritated at the interruption of his sleep and ready to cut
down in anger the idiot responsible. But Martin's appearance and bearing softened his words, and the palace identification which the orderly had never thought to request
brought instant compliance. It did not occur to him that
he was acting without authority of the guardians.

"M'lord," he said deprecatingly, "you will understand
that I have no prior knowledge of this matter."

He was studying the chart and at the same instant trying to keep this powerful personage satisfied that everything possible was and would be done to his desire.
Martin had begun to pace angrily, marking off a space not
much longer than the depth of the cold cell that held the
boy.

"I want a crash team assigned to this," he said. "Your
top priority. Whatever it takes, I want done—an eye trans-
plant, spinal cord restructure, whatever is needed. You
may draw on the Empress's own priority code for contact
approval."

The doctor's estimate of this demanding person went
up several notches.

"There may be irreparable damage, m'lord," he said,
echoing the orderly's words. "The brain may have been
affected."

Martin stopped, pinned him with his eyes. "I hope not,"
he said softly. "This citizen's life is worth at this moment
far more than yours, Doctor. If I were you I would do
everything within my power to repair all damage." There

was the hint of terrible fate to follow failure, although the doctor had no conception of what that fate might be.

"I of course will do everything possible, m'lord."

"I want to know the instant you've made determination," he said. "And under no circumstances is this boy to be assigned to a determination center!" This was a matter that called for investigation as soon as the more pressing problems were out of hand. He wondered how many outside of Stennock's own department were aware that such places existed.

He drew a card case from his cape, scribbled an instant access code across the back of it. "This will reach me at any hour." Then he looked down the length of the room, at the rank of cold cells. "I'd suggest that your first move takes the boy out of this factory—someplace warm. And I want a human present when he wakes, an empath. I don't care where you have to conscript the body."

———◆———

An hour later he was back in the undercity, having stopped long enough to change clothes at an apartment that was not registered to his public identity. Now he belonged to the streets, could blend in without notice everyplace except the palace towers.

There was brief indecision, and then he made cautious contact with a man he used infrequently, and only on matters of the greatest import. Despite the hour the other was awake, ready to do business.

They met near dawn in a cafe close to Old Town, a place popular with slumming upperclasses bored with the dignity of position and neurotic midclasses seeking to establish social contact with their superiors in the only public way permitted. The little man was almost hidden in a shadowed corner booth, and then he turned to greet

Martin, moving into a random light beam, and his face seemed to explode into a blaze of a thousand colors and corruscating shapes. For a few seconds Martin closed his eyes, seeing the dance of brilliant colors against his lids, and when he reopened them the light had shifted again. In the welcome darkness, as his eyes adjusted, he could see that the face paint covered hideous scar tissue.

Even before Martin was in the seat the little man said, "Solomon has been taken by the hounds."

Martin looked around to be sure that there was no one close to them, no real problem at this hour. The cafe was half empty, with more departing at each moment and almost no newcomers taking their place. He brought forth a silence gun, setting it between them and activating it before speaking. Instantly there was the sensation of something heavy falling across his auditory senses and when he spoke his voice seemed curiously flat, as though without emotion.

"I know. I want him back."

A silver ridge shifted, stretching taut a scarlet circle around the eye. The face was void of hair in any position, although it was impossible to tell if the absence was natural or contrived. "He may already be dead."

"I think not. There is too much the hounds would like to pick from his brain. Nor will they wipe him so long as he can convince them that he holds choice information. I think Lord Stennock will keep him alive."

"Even if you are correct in such an assumption, the situation would seem without solution. I know of no one to be rescued from Stennock's private keep."

"Have you located the place?" The question had been asked at every meeting for these past many years, and the quest kept alive the nerve thread that bound them tenuously together. It was a project that had long been subsidized from the Empress's private housekeeping funds, at a great deal of risk to Martin, but he kept the payments coming without protest.

And now the little man grinned, revealing multicolored enameled teeth. Two incisors had been sharpened and now as his tongue moved against them they moved downward, glinting first red and then silver in the uncertain light. He moved his bottom lip behind them, creating in an instant a devil mask that taunted the world of secure souls, and then his lip moved against them again and they slipped back into normal position.

"Yes."

Martin blinked, as though not certain that he had heard correctly, and the little man laughed. "Yes, friend sponsor, I have discovered Lord Stennock's little secret. Although I should keep it to myself awhile yet, permitting you to pay me for the job forever. But it is well completed —Lord Stennock's private quarters are in the palace, no more than a dozen levels removed from the imperial apartments."

The reply was so unexpected that it was shocking. Martin started to speak, then looked up in anger as a waiter came shuffling over with two drinks, mandatory since they had not placed an order. He found small coin and thrust it at the lackey, who pretended indifference to the generator on the table even as it drank the sound of glasses clinking against the plastic surface. He left as insolent as he had come, leaving Martin to let out pent-up breath.

"Are you certain?"

"More so than I am of your motives."

"The arrogance!"

"Lord Stennock is not original in his machinations," said the garish man. "My informant discovered the secret by diligent study of the original engineering specifications for the palace. They are on file if one knows the right place to look—but not in the public areas, of course. It appears that the Prefecture of Police has always maintained private quarters in the palace tower, under the very nose of first the Supremacy and then the Emperors."

"The first Lord of the Supremacy held the police powers in his own portfolio," said Martin. "It was his grandson who saw the power dissipated to the Council. But it answers many questions." He was forced to admire the audacity of the scheme, the man. "I've often wondered how the hounds could disappear so effectively, leaving no trace of their presence in the undercity. I used to think that the secret must be in Old Town. Tell me, do they maintain everything there—the wipe?"

"So it is said. My informant of course could make only educated guesses as to the use put to the various elements of the private levels. You must understand that we have not attempted to actually penetrate the secrets of the seraglio. For myself, I am not anxious to request a guided tour. Of course my informant has forgotten everything."

If the man were still alive. "How many secret levels?"

"Four."

"That seems very few."

"How many do they need? Most of the activities of the police are public."

"How do I get in?"

"Become a guest of Lord Stennock." He leaned back in his corner, resting all ten fingers lightly against the table, head cocked forward so that his chin seemed to disappear.

"Stennock would welcome me in that role," said Martin, "I'm sure. However, there must be an alternative."

"Being as reluctant as you to visit the guardians in their private places, I fear that I could not suggest an easier method. One could always ask for a guided tour, I suppose. Or raise the question of secrecy within the inner councils of the government. However, in that case one must be prepared for embarrassment. It may turn out that the full Council is already aware of Stennock's secret."

"I doubt that. It would not have stayed secret with so many loose mouths. Not all of the Council are in favor of the Prefect, or his policies."

They fell silent for a moment, Martin looking out to where there was a sudden flurry of activity on the tiny dance floor. The other sucked on his sharpened incisor a moment, then yawned, making a show of covering the yawn with a broad gesture of his hand.

"There must be a way," said Martin.

"I am sure," the other replied. "However, the hour is late. I trust we can conclude this business in short order? I would seek my bed."

"Someone on the inside," said Martin. "Who?"

"You are of the palace. You should know every source of disaffection."

"I am of the palace, but not with the currents that swim there. I am in a . . . special, shall we say, position? I am forced to go outside, to people such as Solomon and yourself, to find out what has been happening on the floor below my own apartment."

"A pity," said the little man. "Not that I find regret in that which has proven profitable these past few years."

"There must be someone," said Martin. "You know everything worth knowing—more even than Solomon. Who is the key?"

"You flatter me." He rubbed an ear. "However, you are correct in stating that I pride myself on my familiarity with matters worth knowing, and it could well be that there is just such a person as you suggest. It has been speculated that a certain lady of the palace is in the employ of Lord Stennock, perhaps even in the matter of the wipe itself."

"Her name?" He could not restrain himself from leaning forward, eager now that he was so close.

"Isobel da Canar y Orté."

For the moment the name brought no echoes of a face, a person, and then suddenly there was the image of a woman unnaturally dark, artificially Castilian, in honor of a bloodline attenuated into nothingness even in her husband's family.

"I know who she is, but no more."

"The lady I'bel is not counted among the Empress's confidantes. Not a spat," he said, answering Martin's question before it could be asked. "The paths simply have not crossed—perhaps deliberately."

"I should think Stennock would like to have someone close to the Empress."

"What makes you think he hasn't?"

There was no answer to that uncomfortable question. After a moment the little man went on, "My informant tells me that the lady undoubtedly has a price, albeit a high one. Still, with the royal treasury to draw upon I don't suppose money will be a hindrance."

Martin relaxed now that they were approaching the matter of price. "The Empress does not have unlimited funds—she cannot draw upon the government treasury. The Council treats her generously, but she can go only so far."

"Far enough, I'm sure, even though the lady I'bel is reputed to be extremely greedy. Still, it may be that the price will require little actual cash."

"Services, then."

"The lady married young, an oldster thought then to be in his dotage—a very wealthy oldster, I might add. The marriage was arranged to combine wealth with prestige —it has been said that I'bel changed her name to convince her would-be suitor that they shared common heritage. Still, even with a bloodline two thousand years old or whatever, he was not considered select among the new upperclass of the Supremacy, so he was quite eager to buy her position. But this was many years ago, and the old man has perversely remained alive against all logic and actuarial probabilities. I'bel has tastes expensive far beyond her dowry, but her husband refuses to die and let her enjoy them."

"His fortune has gone into medical support?"

"Not at all—he is naturally long-lived. I understand that he has not yet entered apparent senility, although he certainly approaches the century mark. Really a remarkable man. I trust that the medicians have studied his case well, in the event that I should ever be tempted to remain alive so long."

"Why doesn't she divorce him?"

"There would not be profit enough. She would win support, for she is by nature sympathetic—she may be an empath, which would explain her involvement with the wipe technique. But she must be an unusually cold and heartless talent, for she wants all that her husband owns."

"What, then?"

"The alternative would seem obvious," he said, studying his fingernails.

"Assassination? I am unable to employ the technique."

"Scruples, after surrendering a dozen good men to the mercies of Stennock's mind wipe? You amaze me." He seemed honestly surprised.

"I would always regret the loss of good men," said Martin. "However, those you refer to were bumbling idiots and about to destroy a much larger program. It was necessary to remove them before that happened."

He stared directly at the other but would not say that he was not proud of his own role in the game that had ended last night. He had done only what was necessary, and his greatest regret was that he had brought the boy Tomas into a position of such danger. If his conscience was burdened because of the affair it was not because the fumblers were certain to be transported. They deserved the fate.

There were others, however, who did not . . . such as the lost Solomon. His value against the Council could not be measured in a thousand of the most willing hands. Martin would have traded himself into the mind wipe if it were the only way to save the other.

"You control the assassins in this sector," he said then. "Why haven't you accepted the commission?"

"What would it gain me?" He spread his hands. "If she paid me half what she would gain, it would still only be money. And that is nothing—I have wealth enough that I could not spend it in a dozen lifetimes of pursuing the wastrel. Of itself it means nothing, other than a way to keep score. For that matter, I find that I grow exceedingly bored with this life. Perhaps it is time to choose another way, to die."

"Your mind is too good to lose in death," said Martin. "If you are bored, volunteer for the wipe and transportation. You'll have a new life then."

"Ah, but would I like it any the better? I fear not, and so it is a risk that I do not take."

"Eh, you're nothing more than a barroom lawyer. But if money means so little to you, why accept it so willingly? A great deal has gone from my hand to your account."

"I am simply performing my patriotic duty," he said,

smiling again, the complete terrible grimace, "redistributing the wealth from the organization that has not earned it to one that has. And I do have large expenses, you will admit. It costs dearly to secure that which has been thought not even to exist."

"You do have honor," said Martin. "At least I have never caught you out in a fabrication. Still, if you do not need the palace gold, just what do you gain from this association, from the Empress?"

"My services are available only to those who offer me something that I consider to be of real value," the little man said. "Information, instruction, amusement—these are the goods and chattels that can buy me."

More than that he would not say, leaving Martin to stare blindly at the silence generator even after he was gone, the agent wishing that he could somehow draw the cone of silence about his whole life.

CHAPTER SEVEN

The desert sun was an orange disk streaked with pink as it shone through the thin remnants of haze from the lopal migration. There was no warmth to it now; it seemed to suck all of the heat out of the rock and the sand as it slipped down the horizon, stealing it away from those who needed it most. A bare week ago enough heat had remained at night to keep Aaron comfortable as he passed beyond the confrontation with the great herd, but now they needed their leather tunics and skirts and still huddled together at night.

The people traveled with dawn and with dusk, taking a long break during the day and making less progress than Aaron had hoped. The second day they were forced to stop for the night far from any waterhole. Of itself, that was no problem; they carried water enough for the entire journey, with cautious use. But it was not good for the spirit to stop in the middle of such barrenness. Here even the tiny desert scrub could support no more than three or four plants to each acre. The ground beneath their feet was tortured rock, the only soil a gritty sand that kicked up before the walker with every step, sometimes to be caught by a breeze that would swirl it straight up into the face as though the whirlwind were intelligent in its purpose.

They made shelter for the rest in a wind-carved bowl large enough to harbor three times their number, huddling together in a crack on the southern lip, the three tents almost enough to create the comfortable feeling that they were in a cave and not out on the desert at all. The sunset was brilliant, although perhaps noticeably less so than it had been the night before.

There was little enough to be done at this time, and little spirit to be squandered in banter or casual activity. The men gathered together, the smallest children safe in the center of the circle, as the women began to prepare the supper. Aaron came down to the circle after walking once completely around the rim of the bowl, seeing nothing against the coming night but stray movements of the wind.

"It is cold!" cried one of the old men bitterly. Although his apparent physical age was greater than Aaron's, he was one of the newcomers to the village, arriving perhaps three years before with shoulder twisted and arm nearly useless.

"It is the late season," said Aaron, although there was little enough in this place to separate the seasons one from another. But years, decades, of living with the small movements of wind, rain, and clouds had made him conscious of every one.

"Cold!" James said again, mumbling, moving closer to his neighbor. There was a shift along the circle, spreading away from Aaron's position at the head. He didn't bother to answer the complaint again, bending forward and tucking his head down between his shoulders. It was as though he had always been in this place, as though the others had already forgotten Joseph. Thinking of the old man, even Aaron found that he could not instantly summon the sharp image of his face, and this disturbed him. He felt that it was wrong but he could not put meaning to it and so he forced the thought from his mind.

The sudden cry of a woman brought every man to his feet, hands grasping for something to use as weapon. They looked at each other, not moving, as the cry died quickly on the desert air. Then Aaron was pushing his way through those who blocked his way from the cleft in the rocks, shoving out roughly. A dozen swift paces carried him to the cooking fire.

"What is it?" he demanded, expecting to find that some animal had slipped into the bowl, perhaps even a lopal strayed far from the great pack. But rather than answer, several of the women held out their clenched fists to him, then opened them suddenly, faces wrinkled in disgust. A sour odor struck him, churning his stomach, and he nearly backed away.

"It is all like this!" cried one. "All!"

The grain in their hands was spoiled, infested by larvae that had hatched out during the heat of the day. Aaron ordered the other sacks turned out, only to discover that every last grain was spoiled. The maggots had worked through it all, turning the kernels rancid to the smell and slimy to the touch.

"What are we going to do?" demanded one of the young men. "We are hungry."

"Turn back!" James pushed through two taller men, his twisted shoulder making him seem to lunge with each step. "It is a curse!" There was little the cripple could do for the tribe, although he had some skill in fashioning stone knives. But he was an unwilling worker and would take hours to complete a task that another could do in minutes. Most of the other men would not tolerate him, forcing him to spend his time with the women and the infants.

"The gods have called down their hatred!" he cried

now. "We have defied them and now they will destroy us! We shall die in this forsaken land!"

"Silence!" demanded Aaron, and a near neighbor cuffed James roughly, forcing him to obey. Aaron wiped his hand on his tunic, trying to judge the depth of the fear on the faces that were turned to him. He could not shake the feeling that this was an accursed place to shelter.

But he could not admit this. "The gods are not involved," he said after a moment. "Why should they subject us to torment when we are already following their command? They cursed the land we knew, forcing us to turn away, to follow in their steps."

"How do you know we're going where the gods want us?" cried another. "We may be going in the wrong direction."

"Where, then?" he said. "Would you go north, to follow the lopal? That way lies certain death, and I do not intend to offer my body as sacrifice to such beasts—not I who have killed three of the lopal by myself!"

The questioner lapsed into silence under Aaron's harsh stare, too small to challenge the position of the leader. And it was apparent that none of the others were willing to risk whatever displeasure might come from going against Aaron. But the seeds of discontent had been planted and he knew that the weeds would take close watching else they choke off the good life about them.

He ordered the infested grain burned there, afraid that the insects might somehow find their way across the desert; he even insisted that their garments be turned out, particularly those who had carried the grain sacks, and his caution was rewarded by the discovery of several double handfuls of the maggots hiding in creases and undisturbed corners.

Later, when he was awake long after the others had

drifted into uneasy slumber, grumbling over the hollow places in their bellies, he wondered if the maggots could have been responsible for the failure of the crops at the old village. He had never seen their like before, but they had eaten of the stores yesterday and never knew of the infestation. Perhaps the maggots had been there all along. This same kernel of grain was the food of most of the animals in the old territory, those that did not live exclusively on meat, and if the grain was infected by an unseen plague of the larvae it would make simple explanation why the game animals had been disappearing. It was something that must have been going on for several years, though perhaps just at this time reaching its greatest flood.

His suspicions were not answers but they settled his thoughts and he was finally able to sleep, and even to feel rested when the stirrings of the others indicated that dawn was at hand. The tribe faced three days of hunger, no hardship for the hunters and most of the other young men. But the oldsters and the women suffered, the children forced to be content with the milk of their mothers.

When they stopped that morning, to rest through the day, Aaron sent Rob on ahead as leader of a party of three of the hunters. He had no hopes that they would return with food before the crossing was completed, but it stilled objections of several who were beginning to echo James's grumblings. There was still plenty of water for their needs and enough strong arms to help the weaker ones when they grew faint and stumbled.

They came out of the desert and into the hill country late in the evening of the fifth day since abandoning their old home, leaving an infant and a young man dead in the place of their last night's encampment. Aaron had not been surprised to lose the child but the death of the other had come as a shock. At one moment he had been moving with the others, shouldering more than his share of the burden; at the next he was dead, his heart failing to support him. They could not do for him as they had for Joseph, for there was nothing of which to build a bed, no saplings to support it high above the rock. But Aaron ordered one of the best tent skins wrapped around him, and offered what honor he could. And his sorrow was deeper than when Joseph had willed himself into death, for the young man had no choice in the matter.

The hunters were waiting for them when they came out of the desert, the game they had struck heaped high in a way that few of the people had ever before seen. The feast that followed lasted three long days before Aaron could make them leave off, the men rising with full bellies to dance themselves into a stupor, frenzied with joy, the cycle to repeat itself every few hours. And when it was over they were purged of their sorrows and their doubts, even the constant complainer James coming forward to offer peace with Aaron.

The villagers were willing to stop where they were and live off the bounty of the new land, but Aaron made them cure enough of the meat to last at least a ten-days. When they finally pushed on nearly a fourth of the kill remained to spoil and serve the scavengers who had been afraid to move in against these new creatures. Rob and the other two hunters were proud of their kill and disdainful of the precautions against hunger. What need of dried, aged flesh when all about them the land abounded with creatures easy to capture, to entice into death? Aaron was finally forced to command their obedience, overriding the objections of those willing to stay even though the desert was barely an hour away.

They did move on, however, no matter reluctantly, afraid that Aaron would go without them. Near noon of the next day they came down over the ridge of low hills and found the stream that had nearly killed him, now once again quiet between its banks. Only the high water marks, in some places marking the brush hundreds of yards from the banks, verified his story, and even as he pointed out the landmarks of his adventure Aaron knew that some of the people were finding this new marvel difficult to encompass, added to what had transpired already. It was the young people who seemed to listen now with half an ear, the oldsters accepting every word without question, but he knew that it was the young people that he must hold. And now that they were all well fed again there were one or two who no longer cuffed James away in anger when he came snuffling among them. The cripple seemed to have forgotten his recent vow of allegiance, and though his words never reached Aaron he could see that they were having an effect.

He was resting beneath a tree that evening when Rob came up to him, reluctant to speak. Several of the others were hanging back, even hiding, and Aaron was sure that he saw James among them.

"This is a good land," Rob began hesitantly, stumbling over his words. "It is as good as you said."

"I spoke the truth always."

"The water is good, and shows that it lasts all the year round. There is no evidence that drought has touched this place."

Aaron nodded. "So it is so."

Rob held out his hand. "The land is bountiful, it promises good crops once the women have trained the wild grain to the garden." The words suddenly rushed out. "There are those among us who think that this is the place the gods marked out for us."

Aaron was silent for a moment before answering. Then,

"There is better land ahead. We do not have to settle for the good."

"The people are tired, Aaron!" Rob spread his hands wide. "We have never seen such land as this. We wish to stay."

It was not rebellion, for Aaron knew that they spoke only their honest thoughts. And he could not blame them for wanting to settle for good enough after so many seasons of wanting. And yet he hesitated against their demand, something urging him not to listen. He felt as though the gods were insisting that he continue the journey, that he had traveled too far to accept its ending so readily.

"The gods are wise beyond the powers of men," he said softly. He knew in his heart that he was thinking of himself, not of the people. Reluctantly, ached with the feeling of some great loss, he put the siren call from his mind. He had accepted the burden of the people when he'd accepted Joseph's staff; he could not walk away from them now. And so he accepted that they had come far enough; this would be their new home.

The transformation of the land came quickly; within two weeks there were nearly as many tents as had been in the old place and little sign that the people had not always lived near the river. The hunters moved out every day and soon put themselves out of full-time employment with their success. It was as though the late season never touched this country, the game never migrating and never learning to be afraid of the new creatures. At times it seemed as though the curiosity of the animals had eliminated the need for hunters, for any strong arm could follow the stream out of sight of the tents and return with enough to feed everyone.

Ten ten-days passed, nearly a season, and the people

grew used to their new home; the good became common-
place and even due, the bounty squabbled over not for
possession but for the assignment of duty. The gravid
women delivered their children, all in good health and
not one lost in the first days, while the other females became pregnant again. Another double handful of ten-
days rolled passed, and a third, and the oldest of the
children were underfoot whenever there was serious work
to be done. There was fat on many bodies and idleness
kept too many lazing in the sun. Yet there were no problems to beset the village, no reason why they should not
take advantage of the bounty around them.

Aaron grew away from the people as that year died,
began again to travel out by himself, striking across the
plains or up the stream toward the mountains. He told no
one when he was going, explained his absence to no one
when he returned, and after a time he was not even
missed. Quarrels demanding arbitration could be settled by the opinion of the others, and there was rarely
need to offer justice.

Once Rob asked to go with him, for Aaron was not the
only restless soul in the village, and he agreed. They
stopped three hours away to leave their skirts, then
moved out with only their slings and their wallets, crossing great lengths of the country at a ground-devouring
pace that threatened to leave the younger man far behind.
Aaron could stop only with reluctance, impatiently, then
set out again as soon as the other came up, running as
though all the devils of the sky were after his heels. Three
days he went on in this way, stopping at night only to kill
his food and to sleep, off again with the rising sun, never
explaining to Rob his destination nor his need to hurry
so. The younger man was more than happy when they

finally returned to the village, wondering if Aaron was mad.

Yet he did not always run as though his feet were wings that would carry him through the heavens. There were times when he was content to wander aimlessly, stopping for long rests beside a lake or near the top of an unusually tall hill, searching his soul and his thoughts for the devils that drove him to such torments. There was no peace in him even at those moments, although he could not put name to the things that plagued him so. There was an emptiness in him that refused to be filled.

One trip, halfway through the second year since their arrival at the new country, carried him farther than ever before, across the plains and into a region where the ground complained beneath him and the hills puffed constant smoke. Walking slowly now, fear in his thoughts, he stopped at a spring to refresh himself and scalded his hand in the boiling water. He cursed, nursing the burned side of his hand, and started to draw back. But he could not abandon this which was entirely outside of his experience; he pressed forward, determined to see everything new that this strange land could thrust upon him.

He stopped for the night in a cave, the air hotter than the plains at midday, the sweat pouring from him in the muggy atmosphere. Sleep would not come when he tried to settle himself for rest, his thoughts in turmoil. It was as though the devils were waiting for him just beyond the circle of light cast by his small fire, challenging him to come into the night and meet them on their own terms.

Aaron stared into the night; the cry had come again, hurting his ears with its pain, begging him to come and save the sufferer. His skin crawled and the sweat on his body seemed clammy. His hand stole into the wallet and

touched one of the stones, then his fingers brought forth
his knife, resting the jagged stone on his thigh.

"*Aaron!*"

There, it came again, his name called clearly from the
night. Someone was out there, hurt, someone of his own
people, for how else could they know and call his name?
He shivered, denying his fright but unable to quell the
reactions of his body. He came to his feet, placed most
of his supply of wood on the fire so that it blazed up high,
but the circle of illumination was very little increased.

Was that the cry again? He bent, found a resin-soaked
branch stub that he had set aside for this purpose, and
thrust it into the fire. The torch smoked and gave off a
strange incense but the flame held true even when it was
thrust before him to burn away the darkness. He stepped
cautiously into the night, moving with heavy heart away
from the safety of the fire.

A wind came out of nowhere, smashing the flame of
the torch, scattering resinous sparks into the night, but it
could not put out the flame nor do more than dry the
sweat on Aaron's back. After a minute it died away as
though aware of its failure as the man picked a cautious
way through the night, trying to remember the direction
of the land. A hill was before him and when he circled
around it below him was a bog bubbling slowly with
black oil. The light of the torch struck color in the oil
as a bubble burst and it rippled away.

Aaron did not see the bulk of the wind dreamer until
he was at the very edge of the pool, torch held high over
his head. Then the great creature raised its head, the eyes
catching the torchflame and taking fire from it, burning
through the night with a brilliance that was stronger than
any fueled flame could be.

He stood, riveted by his fear, his only thought that his

soul might flee his body even before he was properly dead. Sweaty fingers held the knife before him as though it could protect him against the monster. His throat caught and he gagged, then forced himself to swallow dry bile. He breathed harshly, lungs fighting for the life in each breath.

When the thought formed in his mind he thought it his own, an expression of the fear that gripped him. But the probe came again and it was as though he was listening to an unintelligible conversation, the words spoken making no sense. He shook his head, trying to clear his thoughts, and brought the back of the fist holding the knife against his forehead. But the question would not be put off, came again, softly insistent.

Who are you?

What are you?

Why are you?

How are you?

You are, who should never be. You, who are not of this place, have come farther than exists. This is not your place, but you are here. I do not understand.

There was pain behind the questing thoughts, for the wind dreamer was aware that it had come to its death. Yet it was as though the pain had been set aside, acknowledged in existence but not important enough to demand the whole attention of the mind.

Who are you?

"Aaron," he said, speaking aloud, his voice a rasp in his own ears. He cleared his throat, spat harshly.

There is more, insisted the other. *I cannot read, for there is a strange barrier that I cannot penetrate. I have never met such as you. There are only my brothers . . . but now there is another. I cannot deny what I behold with my own. . . .*

There was a concept that the man could not accept, tried to thrust away. Then the searching probe began again, touching perhaps more gently now, and he knew that the wind dreamer was examining his very soul. But as the contact was maintained the fear seemed to ebb away and soon was gone as though it had never existed.

There are others, the creature remarked. *I have seen them, three, four, a dozen of them, but I did not know what they were.*

"We are three times that number!" Aaron protested. And then he knew that the other was not referring to the individuals of the tribe. "The others . . . where have you seen them?"

There was a momentary blankness, as though the creature must study the concept of place, then pictures came to his mind in rapid succession: first a deep valley, then an open plain, an ocean's sweep along a broad beach, a place that might have been the original home of his own tribe. There were more, a dozen in all, none of which he could name, know that he had seen.

"Stop!" He was begging. "Are there none close to my own people, near to here?"

Again there was puzzlement, as though near and far were merely different aspects of the same thing, and that a concrete structure. This time the confusion was not resolved, leaving the man frustrated.

You are hurt. The wind dreamer was compassionate.

"No." Aaron shook his head. "I am not hurt." He touched himself as though wanting, needing, to verify his own words.

Not in body, but inside, within . . . Was the missing word "soul"? It was so hard to read what the other was saying. Aaron wanted to fling the torch into the night in his frustration.

You are hurt. It was insistent, a warning that he should not ignore.

"Can you see the place?" he asked. "Can you repair the damage?"

No, for I know not what caused the . . . Again there was a concept that could not make the jump from the other to the man. *It is as though a knife has cut away* . . . *out. We have taken you, I know now that was wrong. We did not know what you are. It shall never happen again.*

There was a sudden wash of bright pain across the back of his eyes. Aaron staggered, dropping both torch and night as he pressed his hands to his face. The torch was at his foot, scorching him, before the pain subsided, letting him realize that he was hurting. He jumped back, howled, and grabbed for his leg.

I come . . .

There was a movement in the darkness and the wind dreamer shifted its bulk, stirring the surface of the bog. One wing lifted temporarily free with a sucking noise, then dropped again in exhaustion. A sigh seemed to fill the night, although Aaron was not sure whether he heard it with his ears or with his mind.

I die.

He panicked. "No! Wait—you can't die now. Wait, morning will be here soon. I can get you out of there. I can go for help—"

I have stayed too long. I will pay for my . . . There was the sensation of a maelstrom. *I must answer to that which is over. I wish I could help you, but I am done. My clan brothers know you, Aaron-creature called man. I have taken you, not knowing that you were* . . . Alive? It was the only word that made sense. *It will not happen again. There is little enough like us, there shall be no less.*

The feeling of loneliness was so sharp that he knew

tears were filling his eyes, and was without shame. There was a sense of irreplaceable loss and he could not now imagine that he had ever feared such a creature.

He called to the great thing, but there was only one more response. *I . . . sky master . . .* Even as the concept faded away from his forethoughts, he was aware that the wind dreamer was dead. He sank to his knees, thrusting the torch into the soft ground at the edge of the bog, and closed his eyes, beseeching the gods to take him in place of this magnificent creation. But as usual the gods would not respond, even though the flame of the torch guttered out, leaving the man alone in a darkness that was empty even of the stars in the skies.

CHAPTER EIGHT

The public corridors of the palace were never still, the pace of activity continuing constant throughout every twenty-four-hour span. There were differences in kind, of course; most of the late night traffic was service functionaries. Thus the raven-haired lady of the palace seemed out of place when she came out into one of the great hallways. None of those who saw her, however, would have dared question her presence even if they could find reason to speak directly to her person.

I'bel stopped before a level directory, hands resting on the railing of the service console before it. No one could see the identification sliver that was cupped in her left hand, nor know that a minute blood sample was taken and analyzed in that brief few seconds even as an unseen eye probed and made a retina imprint, comparing all of the diverse snippets of information against the master file that was located in the police levels.

Satisfying the monitors that she was neither fraudulent nor controlled, she moved next to an unremarkable lift that would take her to the private levels of the guardians. The apparent maintenance technie on the board had scarcely seemed to glance at the regal woman, although I'bel was astonishingly attractive in a milieu of unusual beauty, living her days among those who had raised the cosmetic art to its highest and most creative level. She seemed bored now; it was not necessary for her to indicate a destination for that had been done for her by her method of approach.

————◆————

At five o'clock the previous afternoon she had arrived at the entrance to the Empress's private apartments, not quite believing that she had been invited to a private tea with Karyn herself. There were other guests, of course—four of Karyn's oldest and dearest friends. It happened that one of those was one of the few known to be intimate with I'bel de Canar, who saw nothing untoward in being urged to invite her aloof friend.

The summons to the tea had come at noon, upsetting two of the invitees who found that they would have to make last-minute changes in their plans for the evening. I'bel was honored by the invitation, however; she had seen the Empress only at a distance, at public functions. Even on the few occasions when she had been to a palace ball she had come no closer than arm's length to the Empress. It did not distress her to make hurried arrangements for the party, for there was nothing so important in her tedious life of waiting for her husband to die that a palace invitation would not take precedence.

The party was cozy, Karyn at her most charming although there were those who claimed that the Empress would be vindictive when the mood struck. But she was showing only her good side now. An hour passed in inconsequential chatter and when it ended the stranger of the guests had been flattered to find that most of the royal attention had been directed to herself. That drew no special notice from the others, for they had assumed that Karyn had called the tea in a fit of boredom; it was only natural that she should explore the newest personality to the fullest. They were therefore not surprised when Karyn asked I'bel to stay a few moments longer when the others had been dismissed.

--------◆--------

The lift carried her now to a corridor that might have been any similar hallway in the public part of the palace tower. Only the most observant might have noticed that there was no identification of the level over the lift entrance and an absence of the constant ebb and flow of palace humanity.

I'bel turned to her left and passed a dozen closed doors and then one that stood open, revealing the rather cramped quarters of a public counselor. She recognized the man within, having worked with him before; she wondered what role he was playing at the moment.

Shortly thereafter she entered two successive side corridors and then was at a set of closed double doors that blocked the hallway. There was a guardian here as well, but in uniform this time, and it was necessary to go through the process of identification once more. Then the doors ponderously slid open to her, for they were cored with a full inch of high-carbon steel and sheathed in a ceramic used in the combustion chambers of nuclear rockets. Lord Stennock had been assured that his chambers were secure against any attack short of nuclear; the doors had been guaranteed to stand thirty minutes against the highest-powered laser. They also were locked with a dozen separate devices, each independent of the other and able to stand alone against any reasonable explosive attack.

Once beyond the barricade I'bel found herself in a rather prosaic clinic, walls painted hospital green, the three chairs in the little waiting area coldly plastic and chrome. A matronly woman was at the desk, apparently intent on a personal view screen below the level of the railing. She looked up, flustered, to see I'bel before her, as though she had not been aware of the process of entry.

"Oh, dear! You startled me, m'lady. What brings you here at this hour? We have nothing scheduled, do we?" She was looking anxiously for a possible warning slip among the clutter on her desk.

"Nothing scheduled," said I'bel. "It's a dull evening, I couldn't sleep. I thought I'd come and take another crack at the fat pig."

"Oh, of course." But she still seemed worried. "You do have authorization . . . ?"

As though bored with the nonsense of routine I'bel produced the pass that admitted her to Solomon's room —altered by Martin to give her twenty-four-hour access. Her stomach unknotted when the nurse accepted it without checking against the original file, the woman nodding in relief.

"He's a stubborn one, that one," the woman said. "I overheard one of the doctors discussing him with the monitors." Now she seemed embarrassed to have to admit that she listened to private conversations. But there was no other way that the information could have come to her and it was too good to keep to herself. "They think the probe is going to be useless, that he should go straight into the wipe. I must say, I'll be happy when they finish with him. The sooner he's transported, the better for all of us—and for my peace of mind."

"Has he been flirting with you?" I'bel asked dryly.

"What? Oh, no, m'lady!" She shook her head vehemently. "Nothing so common as that—I wouldn't have that from such as him!" She reddened. "It's just that he . . . disturbs me. There seems to be an aura, such a cold feeling around him. I don't know why—sometimes I feel as though I should turn him loose, help him get out of here. Not that I ever would think of doing such a thing," she added hurriedly.

"Of course," agreed I'bel. "He's a broadcaster, an uncommonly strong one. Too bad they didn't pick up on his talent in childhood."

The nurse sniffed. "He says he's never had a childhood. The idea!"

"Perhaps he didn't," said I'bel. She knew that Solomon had been born in Old Town, never registered. God knew what those animals did in their squalor. Certainly no life that came from that sink could be considered normal.

There were half a dozen small patient rooms across the corridor, and to the left an operating theater. To her right was a dressing room and she went there now to change into a smock. She did not bother to try to disguise her elaborate hairdo, however; she had suffered too long in sitting for it to risk destroying it now, no matter what the motive.

Now that she had circumvented the first obstacle she calmed down, but before she left the dressing area she faced herself in the mirrored wall over the counter, leaning forward with her weight on the ends of her palms. She looked deep into her own black-flecked eyes, the pupils gray in this artificial light, forcing herself to go through the complete range of mental exercises that would relax her mood, calm her deepest thoughts. Only then, when she had finally purged herself of emotion, was she ready to face the man down the hall.

A bribe from the Empress was so completely outside of I'bel's experience that for several moments she sat in silence, staring at Karyn. Bribery of itself was not apart from her normal life; she used it herself frequently and on every level. To this moment, however, her most persuasive efforts had failed to win her that one thing she most desired.

To have it offered now, without asking . . .

"M'lady, I . . . don't know what to say," she finished, embarrassed, the last words rushing out.

"You value your freedom?" asked Karyn.

"Above all else," she agreed. "But what you ask . . . the very fact that you ask it . . . you force me into a situation that is"—she shrugged—"delicate?"

Karyn laughed and reached to pour herself another glass of wine. "Yes, the matter is delicate. But of great value. I offer you succession to your husband's estates. In return, I ask only for . . . cooperation. A matter of days, perhaps only hours—certainly little enough to give to win in return everything you most desire."

I'bel could not deny the reasonableness of the request. "Your offer is most generous, m'lady," she said. "But . . . the risks may be greater than you anticipate. It is dangerous to go against the will of the Council."

The embarrassing truth lay before them, that Karyn was Empress in name only, without real power. There was silence as I'bel stood against her, their eyes locked. It was not Karyn who dropped away first.

"It may be," she said then, "that matters will not always be as they are now. In times past my grandfathers held absolute control over the Supremacy and the Empire. The Council served only as their advisors. That day may well come again, and sooner than you think."

I'bel stared again, in disbelief. Was the Empress actually talking treason?

"These walls are secure," said Karyn, amused. "I have my own technicians to serve me, protect me, and I am

certain of their loyalties. The Council has no entry here
. . . and I am certain, m'lady, that you would not want
word of this discussion to leave these rooms."

God's truth, yes! I'bel blanched a moment, then shook
her head. "I cannot help you, m'lady. I would, but you
ask the impossible."

Karyn and Martin had discussed the possibility that
fear might force I'bel to react in the way exactly opposite to their needs. There was no easy solution to the
problem and finally it was decided that the game would
have to play its own way out. He had been waiting elsewhere in the apartment, overhearing everything that had
been said since the beginning of the party. Now that it
was obvious that I'bel was slipping through their fingers,
he came into the room. . . .

I'bel paused outside of the clinic room, willing her
mind to go completely blank. As she forced away her own
thoughts others came drifting to impinge on the surface
of her mind: a worry over a sore that would not heal that
came from the nurse at the desk; a release of unexpected
violence as a clerk threw a spoiled report against a wall;
a concern with the repair of a uniform before inspection
that was the guard within the room; self-pity that was
churning hatred that came from someone too young to
know such self-consuming hatred. She did not actually
read the thoughts but they merged with her sensitive
overmind and concentration would have brought meaning from the emotions.

Then, as she tuned in on his sleep patterns, other intrusions ignored and shunted aside, there was a combina-
tion of anger/amusement/tolerance from the man called
Solomon.

I'bel resented giving of herself, the employment of her talent by others of the government, but she had no say in the matter. Sensitives were a rare occurrence in this age. They were not permitted to refuse service, conscripted as soon as their talent was recognized. Those of the lower classes, the citizens, were forced to give their entire life to their talent. I'bel was of higher birth and able to control most of her life, but she was required to give so many hours in a year. Her empathetic reaching out for others was noted in early childhood, and from that day on her training had been concentrated on the exercise of that one ability. Perhaps it was only natural that on other, more private levels she came to hate those around her and above her, and even in time to hate herself.

But her talent was too strong to be willed away no matter how her public personality developed. She was able at an early age to wall off that surface world from her core mind, to reach out and take in what others could never vocalize. At the moment when her services became useful she was given by lot to the guardians, to the Prefect of Police, and ever since she had served the mind wipe process on its many levels. She approached those duties without emotion, caring nothing for the victims of the process, even resenting them for the intrusion into her private time. Her talent permitted her entry into their confidences so long as she disguised her own lack of interest.

The guard stood as she entered the room although he had been equally at attention in his chair, arms folded in prescribed manner across his chest, feet flat on the floor, knees an approved six inches apart. The light level was at day normal, permitting no shadow to fall across the bulk of the man in the bed.

Solomon was physically restless in sleep; he had managed to disturb his bedclothes, one sheet pulled clear away from the mattress, the other barely covering one lower leg. Although the humidity was controlled tiny droplets of sweat were scattered across the creases in his face. He wore only the bottoms of his hospital pajamas, naked from the waist up. I'bel stood beside him for a moment, watching the rippling of the obscene tattoos as his pendulous breasts heaved with every shallow breath.

She reached for his mind then, touched it, and found only cold blankness that mirrored back her own probing. His control was superior; he had stood firm before the probe of the strongest sensitives that Lord Stennock could send against him, not weakening even when they were linked together, a dozen in tandem.

But she was not trying to penetrate those defenses now; I'bel had brought a message from Ducas Martin. She touched his shoulder, the contact an electric tingle, and closed her own eyes as she concentrated on him. And the message entered, let in through the defensive globe, accepted and understood. His eyes opened then as though he had not been asleep after all, and there was the suggestion of a smile on the corner of his lips. Then he astonished her by closing one eye in a wink that could not be other than obscene.

I'bel stepped back, surprised, and turned as though to speak to the guard. He was taken unaware when she broke the stun capsule before him, the tiny wisp of gas paralyzing him instantly. His posture kept him erect, eyes opened and staring, so that a monitor making casual inspection of his screen might not notice anything out of the ordinary. But she knew that she had at best only minutes before the guard's brain was affected by the loss of oxygen. If the antidote were not given he would be a vegetable in seven minutes, dead in ten.

She turned back then, leaning over Solomon's bed and placing her fingertips against his forehead as though attempting to aid her probing. Her lips did not move; only her throat revealed the words she was sounding out for him. Martin's message was simple and took less than a minute to relay in its entirety. But even as she gave it I'bel was aware that her heartbeat was increasing, her conditioning slipping. She rushed the last words and hurried to straighten, willing her heart to be still. Solomon nodded once, a tiny movement almost unnoticeable in the normal heaving and shifting of his bulk as his body responded to the needs of lungs and other organs. As soon as she was sure that he understood everything she turned and snapped another capsule before the guard.

That one blinked and then sneezed and was instantly red with embarrassment at being caught out in such a normal reaction to an irritant in his nasal membrane. I'bel refused to look at the ceiling, certain that the monitor had noted and marked out the sneeze as something worth checking on. Even now the guardians must be approaching, perhaps were already in the hall outside, but she moved with measured slowness to the door and opened it, only her training making it possible for her to leave the room as though nothing but routine had transpired during a normal visit.

Even in the dressing room she was unable to relax completely, aware that her fingers were trembling although her fears of instant detection had proven baseless. She was sure that the nurse at the desk had followed her with prying eyes, ignoring the woman's duty to do no other. She needed a relaxant and found cigarettes that someone had forgotten in a drawer. She broke the shield and puffed the stale tobacco into life, coughing as the dry smoke rasped her throat. But almost immediately the cigarettes worked their desired effect, a soft lassitude spreading over her and calming her body, reducing the pace of her heartbeat as the drug slipped into her bloodstream.

It was only then that she dared change clothes, check makeup to be sure that nothing had slipped during the moments of tension, and leave, no longer worrying that the nurse's eyes were burning holes through her back.

Martin paced a measured thirty yards of the gallery that overlooked Old Town, rage flooding his bloodstream with adrenalin. At every swing of the post he glanced at his watch and then to where the light from the undercity came out to mingle unsuccessfully with the garish glory that overlaid the ancient city ruins. This was the place where he had brought Tomas, and the same guard was in position at the top of the stairs. But now in place of the truncheon he carried a studded club, wicked but homemade, and no badge of honor for that reason. He wondered if the man still owed allegiance to Solomon or if he had already sworn to a new master.

He had attracted attention from several of the Old Town denizens as they slipped through the night but none dared approach him closely, recognizing the violence that was barely constrained and not knowing what manner of arms he might be carrying for protection. He had been here nearly an hour now, well past the time planned, and his anger was as much to cover his fear that Stennock's hounds had uncovered everything as for any other reason.

She came then, wearing a shapeless brown cloak that masked her identity and even her sex, although no one with eyes could have mistaken her for anything but a woman by the way she walked. She hung inside until she attracted the idle attention of two loafing guardians and then she scurried out too quickly, sure to rouse their suspicions. But they did not follow her into the sanctuary even though the Guard was perfectly free to arrest wherever they wished, even in Old Town itself.

"You reached him?" he demanded.

She nodded, then spoke huskily. "Yes. There were no problems. But I must have the pass altered back to avert suspicion tomorrow . . . today."

He accepted it, slipped it within his own cloak. "Two hours and I'll have it sent to your door."

"I hope Lord Stennock does not request my presence before that."

"Why should he? Stennock was never a creature of the night—only his hounds act best in darkness. He prances brave in the sunlight, where he can seek the fullest glory of his deeds."

"Something could still go wrong."

"Don't worry. You've handled your part perfectly so far. I've reached the technician you indicated, and I'm sure he'll play the game our way. With the two of you on the spot, nothing can go wrong."

"Everything could go wrong," she said bitterly. "I wish that I were out of this."

"You'll have your reward, m'lady," reminded Martin.

"Little good it will do me, struck under the probe and wiped! All of the estates of Earth will be worthless when I am transported."

"That cannot happen if you keep sensible."

"I don't want to be transported," she said. "To live as an animal, naked—what life is that? I'd rather face death here, among my own. I should have gone straight to Lord Stennock when you proposed your dirty business and had done with it—and with you."

"The Empress could not have allowed it," he said softly. "The death of a lady of the palace would be a great embarrassment, and very difficult to explain, but we would have found a way."

I'bel shivered. What manner of man was this? At this moment she felt in him a coldness that was not human. Could he be a man at all, or perhaps a sport, transported here from another world where men were strange things and not to be pitied?

Fueling his own despair, Martin carried with him the image of a visit earlier that night to the clinic where the body of Tomas had been removed. It was only a body, although his orders had been carried out to the letter and the boy was out of cold sleep. But he lay as dead, not responding even to the touch, the presence, of his only friend.

The empath sharing the boy's room was an aging man, a citizen from his manner; he shrugged in embarrassment as answer to Martin's unspoken question.

"His mind—I cannot touch him, m'lord." The man spoke in sorrow, feeling his own failure deeply. Unlike I'bel, he became a part of the lives he touched. "There is nothing, nothing at all, either on the surface or deep beneath. It is as though the mind never was."

For this Stennock would pay!

"I must leave. . . ." But before she could move away from him a figure was slipping through the darkness, then coming close. He tensed, seeing the man half a minute before I'bel knew that he was on the gallery; then he relaxed as he recognized his informant.

"The hounds are loose," said the garish man without preliminary. "They strike across the entire city."

"Who is their target?"

The hairless eyes stared somberly. "You."

Martin stiffened and could not resist the impulse to spin around, as though they were there already.

"The word went out nearly an hour ago," said the garish man. "They thought you were in the palace. They've only now come out into the streets."

Martin reached into his cloak and retrieved I'bel's pass, thrusting it back into her hands. "Here, take it. Use it with caution, try not to let it out of your hands when you pass it for examination."

"I can't!"

"You must," he said. "There is no choice. You know what must be done, and you have the technician. You know that we will not permit failure, so consider this as though it were you under the wipe and not Solomon!"

I'bel moved away from him then, restoring the pass to a safe place, then darted swiftly between two pillars and from their sight.

"She hates you," said the garish man. "But she is afraid of you and that is enough. She will do as you want."

"Are you empath?" demanded Martin, not surprised.

"I could have been," the other said softly. Then, "Go! Get away while there is still time."

Martin touched his hand briefly, the first time in their years of acquaintance that he had performed this act of friendship, and then he was moving for the stairs. Even as he thrust past the guard with a coin for his demanded toll the light coming from the undercity was changing, waxing blue, warning the people to stop where they were.

The garish man watched Martin out of sight, then moved a little way further along the gallery. When he stopped it was to attach something to the railing. Then he swung himself up and over, hanging there against the bulk of the city until the guardians spilled out onto the gallery. Then he let himself fall into the night.

CHAPTER NINE

The day he returned from witnessing the death of the wind dreamer Aaron knew that he must move away from the village. He came with the sun, gathered only those things essential to a solitary hunt, and within minutes was ready to leave. Then Rob came out of the morning shadows, hanging back as though afraid to approach.

Aaron stopped, his burden contained in a single small pack. He had made no attempt to strike his tent or add anything that could hinder free movement—only Joseph's staff was in his hand, alien though it was to what he had allowed himself. Now as he looked toward Rob he struck the staff into the soft ground.

"I am going."

Rob nodded. "Will you be back?"

He had not thought of the future, of what he would need to do tomorrow. "I don't know. I will come, yes, but I cannot say that I will stay."

"The people need a leader."

"They do not need me," he said. "I have not been leader since the day we first came to this land. The people did as they wished, chose their own way. I did not want to stay then."

"We followed you across the desert. We would follow you again."

"Why? Where? I do not know where I am going—I

only know that I must go. I am not the one to watch over them."

Rob was obviously troubled but Aaron was not sure that he really wanted him to stay. He held out his hand at his waist, looking down to watch his spread fingers. Then he looked back to Aaron.

"Help us choose another."

"Here." He touched the staff again, pulled it from the ground and held it toward Rob. "This can choose your leader. With the staff in your hand, you will be the leader."

Rob stared at the staff, came forward only far enough to accept it in silence, then fell back again. Aaron moved forward a step, wanting to clasp hands in friendship, then stopped again, reluctant, afraid to force himself on the other, afraid that to make the first move would be to bind himself to the people.

"If we need you, what shall we do?"

The question embarrassed him, showed that Rob could not understand his motives—and the embarrassment came because he himself did not know the reasons behind his actions. He shrugged. "You will not need me. If you speak to the sky, to the ground, if there is good reason, then I will hear. I will come."

And then there was nothing more to say. He had not mentioned the wind dreamer, did not tell Rob that the great creatures were sentient, could perhaps be helpful to men. That knowledge was only for himself, to be hoarded even though greed for something so important was a shameful emotion. He recaptured the step, moving backward slowly as he cast one final look at the village. A number of the people were about, moving lazily through morning routine, but none were paying attention to the two men.

Then he turned, moving silently, feet gliding swiftly over the ground and the grass. He knew no special destination but he was anxious to leave this place. Even before he was away from the village his pace was quickening, driven to speed by a madness that set him against himself. He was a runner who had crossed the great desert, crossed the plains, crossed everything that had been set against him, and still he was running, as though he were trying to reach the end of the world.

The hours passed without notice as his feet pounded over the ground, his heart swelling in his chest as he fought for the strength-giving breath that would let him keep moving forever. Never had he run so fast, not even when crossing the desert at the time of the lopals, when he'd thought that the very demons were at his heels. He forced himself to ever greater effort until at last his ears rang with the singing of his blood and his eyes blurred as they sunk low in their sockets. He took no notice of the land around him, of the sky wheeling through the endless circle of day and night, nor even of the pain as he forced his body to work beyond any human demand. The breath was drawn flat now through his nostrils, lips peeled back against teeth that were tight clenched against his tongue. Each blow of his foot against the ground was a shock that stung through his heels and his calves, the pain darting upward to add to the toll taken against his pounding chest, but he ignored the demands that were sounding through his flesh and his bones, ignored the singing in his blood and his ears and his brain, intent only on the run that was taking him away from bondage and out to freedom.

And then it was gone, all at once, the strength and the breath and the vision, everything deserting him and leaving him to collapse in one movement, legs and arms and

even head flailing wildly, rolling and tumbling as he was
carried down the slant of a hill, rocks and thorns striking
out to draw the agonized blood until he ended up in an
untidy heap against a copse of low bushes at the bottom
of the slope.

His heart continued to pound wildly as he lay there,
unable even to straighten himself, to remove one hand
from under his back, to shift in any way from the terrible
discomfort of the position. He was staring up at the sky
but his vision was marred by the foliage of the bush moving against the corner of his eye, distracting him from
the clear beauty of the heavens. His stomach burned and
his loins seemed filled, but he ignored the pain, the aching, the warning signals of his body, pushing them away
until they were gone in a haze that had crept up on all
sides, surrounding him and wrapping him in a false comfort that promised to soothe away the terrible hurting in
his body and his soul.

He slept. . . .

----------◆----------

During the long hours of sleep, when his body gave in
to the limitations of flesh, the demon was stilled. His flesh
ached in every fiber and there was pain in his gut that
was almost an explosion when he came awake, driving
away every other thing in the universe until he answered
the physical demands of his body; but when he was at
last able to move away from the bush and sit up the madness was gone, the need to run into complete insensibility
satiated. The sky was brilliant with the early night stars,
the ground painted with dew that served to quench his
thirst. Then he wiped the cool moisture across his face
and on the insides of his arms and legs.

Aaron had no way of knowing how long the mad flight

had lasted, how many hours he had driven himself beyond normal exhaustion, but he had come a long way from the village. He would never be able to recover the territory in a single day, perhaps not in two. As he chewed on a bit of dried meat from his sack he knew that he was in a place completely new to him. It was a land of low rolling hills, broken occasionally by outcroppings of the basic building material of the continent. In the distance, still ahead of him, the low bulk of table mesas loomed against the night horizon. He had never seen their like before and they were enough to mark the strangeness of this new land.

It was painful for his teeth to work over the scrap of meat; he swallowed it as soon as possible and stood, bending to massage his thighs. Then he forced himself to walk a bit, away from the hill, as the overburdened muscles eased back into normal movement. His odor was strong in his own nostrils and he sniffed the night air, trying to detect the presence of water. But nothing came to him, not even the spoor of recent dung. It was as though this country was empty of life. He could not know by night, but he had come further than ever before, the mesas ahead growing from an offshoot of the main desert that had found a split in the mountain barrier.

Despite the achings in his body Aaron was slept out. He made his way up the hill in the hopes that it would offer him a vantage point, but there was little to be seen here even after his eyes adjusted to the demands of the night. He cleaned his ears with his little finger and cleared his nasal passages, but the added sensitivity brought nothing.

Then he opened his mind to the sky, remembering how the wind dreamer's cry had come to him, and after a time there was a touch from some place far away, a sliding passage that was gone almost before grasped and then returning again as its maker was intrigued. Even then it was brief greeting . . . *Aaron man-creature* . . . but he knew that he had contacted one of the sky master's clan brothers. Even though he had divorced himself from his own kind he was not alone. He would never be alone again.

Then, against the distance, he saw the tiny spark of fire. It flickered low against the darker bulk of the land so that it was not directly on the horizon, and would disappear for several seconds, once for more than a minute; then it would show again, a dance of yellow that he knew must be controlled.

Who else was in this place? It could not be someone from the village for they could never have followed him this far—and the hunters there would never make so strenuous a journey when there was all the game they could desire within minutes of the village. Aaron did not think that a one of them had been an hour away from the village in the past year.

It must be men, for the creatures of the world had never learned to control fire. Excitement hastened the pace of his heart and he dropped to a crouch, supporting himself against overbalancing with the tips of his fingers against the ground as his eyes peered into the darkness, fixing for certain the place of the fire. He had first crossed the desert two years ago because Rob had thought he had seen strange men. Rob had not been bold enough to come away from the desert's edge to follow them, and so they had been lost.

Were these the same ones Rob had seen? Or someone else again, one of the dozen groups the wind dreamer could remember seeing in its solitary flights that had carried it many times across the world?

It made no difference; Aaron was on his feet then, moving out into the night, his aches and discomforts forgotten in the new excitement. He was heading straight for the beacon fire, forced to move more cautiously than during the mad flight of yesterday, but the ground slipped by rapidly beneath his feet as he set a pace that called for a minimum of waste motion. He crossed a great open space that was covered only with wild grass, empty of any life larger than the tiny burrowing creatures, and in less than an hour the ground was rising before him, broken now by occasional hillocks and mineral outcroppings. Deeper shadows in an occasional rocky place showed the presence of caves.

The others had taken advantage of just such a cave for their shelter for the night. It was in a good location, perhaps thirty feet above the level of the ground and reachable only along a narrow ledge that was twice man-length long. Aaron held back from the circle of light, the fire built on the rim of the ledge to keep the smoke away from those within, watching the single man visible. The stranger was chewing on a small bone, and now from long experience he dropped the finished fragment into the fire rather than throw it out into the open where it might entice an unknown predator to come out of the night.

The guard was only a youth, as beardless as Aaron and scarcely more than a boy. It had been a long time since Aaron had seen anyone of his years. There had been a few as young when he had first come into awareness, but they had aged. And the children of the village were years away from this stage of their life.

Something attracted the guard's attention then, and he rose from his crouch and moved back into the cave, then came forward again with a spear in his hand. Aaron did not recognize the instrument, although he understood the reasoning for the short blade that was fixed to the shaft, the polished stone catching the light of the fire and glit-

tering it back into the night. But there was more, a hook-
shaped piece of wood held loosely in the other hand,
fastened to the guard's wrist by a leather thong. Now the
hook dangled free as he held his hand over his eyes, trying to see beyond the fire and into the night. Whatever
had disturbed him was not repeated, and after a moment
he relaxed and stepped back into the cave, coming out
to resume his position without his weapons.

Aaron settled himself into the watch, staying in that
one position for more than an hour. The guard rose once
more to move along the ledge, then went back into the
cave and his place was taken by another, older man. Once
that one had settled himself solidly Aaron stood, eased
the tension from his legs, then moved back and around in
a wide circle that brought him out above the cave, on
the crest of the hill. He worked his way forward from
there, once dislodging a pebble that seemed to clatter
down the slope with unnatural loudness in the dark; he
froze, not moving a muscle for the space of a hundred
breaths. Only then, when there was no indication that
the noise had been heard in the cave, did he let himself
crawl forward again, cautious only because it was the
night and sensible men would challenge anything that
came out of it. And these strangers were sensible, perhaps even fearful.

His efforts were for nothing, however, for he could not
get far enough over the break of the hill to see the ledge.
And so he cradled his head in his arms and willed himself into the sleep that would help pass the long hours of
waiting till dawn.

⸻◆⸻

He came awake instantly, before the grass beside him
had faded from blackness to gray, and retraced his steps

backward, on all fours, until he was over the crest of the hill. Then he rose to his feet and came down to the level of the cave. There were two men standing there now, one kicking out the fire as the sky found its first color of the morning, and then the youth came out of the blackness that was the cave and moved along the ledge to relieve himself. Then the three were coming down off the ledge, burdened far more heavily than Aaron.

While waiting in the darkness he had considered the many possible ways of approaching the strangers, rejecting most of the schemes out of hand. These were hunters like himself; it would not do to take them by surprise, for the repayment could be unexpected death. It would be best to let them make the discovery, come upon him, and so he circled around them again after making sure of their direction of travel and moved out ahead. One hill lay astride the trail that they must take and there he took a stand, to wait for them.

The sun climbed until its heat was baking the land before the strangers came into sight, moving at a leisurely pace that indicated no need to hurry. They saw Aaron instantly, for the eyes of a hunter must be sharp, and stopped; then they were falling back out of sight. Several minutes passed during which they did not reappear, but Aaron knew that they were watching him.

The wait was longer than he had expected but he had chosen his position well; they could not come upon him here by surprise and to circumvent the position would force them far back and around. He did not think their curiosity would let them do that.

He was rewarded for his patience, although not for a goodly chunk of an hour; then the three came forward together, still whispering until they were close enough to call to him. Then they fell silent, stopping perhaps a hundred paces below him.

"We don't know you!" called one.

Aaron spread his hands wide to show that he was unarmed and made a half shrug.

"I am a man," he said.

"You are not one of the people," said the same man. "Have the gods made a sending while we have been away?"

"I am not of your village," Aaron replied. "I come from across the plain, from another village. My people are in the hills near the ending of the desert."

"Why are you here, in our territory?"

He had known that their natural caution would make them suspicious, for it was only by examining with skepticism every new thing that a hunter could stay one step ahead of the gods. But even cautious curiosity burned strong and they were incapable of leaving off the unusual. They would take every opportunity to examine the new, particularly when there was no apparent harm in one man standing against three.

Aaron turned to let his hand take in the landscape, bleak even in day despite the widespread grass. "Do you claim this as territory? Nothing can live here, there is no game worthy of the name. To live here a man would have to learn to eat air."

"There is no game this close to the desert," admitted the spokesman for the others. "But this land belongs to our people."

"What good is land that is worthless?"

The question was disturbing, for they had no answer. Instead, the man said, "There have been no other people here before this day, but now you have come. Why?"

"It is my way," said Aaron. "I come because it is my

need to see what has not been seen before. I did not know
that there were people here, but now that I have seen you
I am glad. I would have our peoples meet, perhaps even
join together."

"Why?" the hunter demanded again.

"How many are you?" They looked at each other in
puzzlement but did not answer. Aaron said, "There are
four double handfuls in my village, which is enough to
satisfy the requirements of our need. But it is long now
since the gods placed me here, and in my days I have
seen the sickness that can destroy an entire village. I
have seen my people nearly destroyed, with only a single
handful of men left. In our number we are weak, but if
the two villages were together it would be hard even for
the gods to strike against that many."

The spokesman nodded, satisfied with Aaron's words.
"You speak truth. You will come with us?"

"Yes." He did not add that it would be necessary for
them to break his leg to prevent that very happening. He
scooped up his pack and came down to them, letting
them examine him closely as he approached. They wore
cloth wrapped around their loins and were disturbed by
his nakedness; the apparent leader found a spare garment
in his belongings and gave it to Aaron. He accepted it,
studying the unfamiliar stuff closely, rubbing it between
his fingers, then followed their example in wrapping himself. Although he kept his opinion to himself, he thought
his own people's leather tunics far more practical, should
a garment be necessary.

The strangers did not travel as Aaron, always running,
but their pace was fast enough to swallow the land
quickly now that they were bearing something of interest.
Before long they were moving through more bountiful
territory, stopping at midday beside a shallow lake to

refresh their thirst. Aaron saw fish jumping a short way from shore and the boy produced his spear, fitting it into the hook of the other mysterious device, then waded out until the water was at his knees. He hesitated for a moment, then used the hook-thing to throw the spear down into the water, the shaft moving so quickly that Aaron could not have said the instant between leaving the hook and quivering in the muck at the bottom of the lake. When the boy retrieved it he brought with it a wriggling silver-red body.

"Hah!" He splashed toward them, slipping the fish from the spear and throwing it onto the shore, then returning three times more to repeat his performance. Even before he was finished with the catch one of the others had built a small fire, while the other stripped rushes, using them as spits after the fish were gutted. The spokesman found a twist of salt in his baggage, which made Aaron marvel even more than he had at the marvelous spear, and they settled to a satisfying meal.

They lazed for an hour in the heat of midday, staying there beside the small lake. The boy dove into the water, then challenged Aaron to join him and for a time they sported while the others slept. But the others came awake instantly, without warning, ready to take the trail again.

They were climbing through a hilly area again by the middle of the afternoon, the rocks heaved up until they were forced to pick a cautious way through a series of gulleys that had never known rivers. They were passing single file through a particularly tortuous path when he heard the snarl directly overhead. He froze against the rock, craning up to see a beast half man-size and crouched for leaping. Even as the others were adjusting their spears and trying to judge placement, almost impossible in this confined space, Aaron's hand went to his wallet and retrieved sling and stone. There was not enough room and so he shortened his swing, but when the stone flew its path was straight and true, striking the beast as it rose from its ledge, forelegs already traveling out in its leap.

It hung there a moment, suspended in eternity, its cry of triumph choked off; then it was tumbling forward, crashing off the rocks to land almost at Aaron's feet. The one eye was open and staring at them in yellow hatred, but the stone had smashed across its nostrils and caught the other eye square. Blood began to gather slowly in the ruined socket and to trickle from the corner of the mouth.

The proficiency with an unknown instrument of death brought immediate acceptance, any suspicions of Aaron gone. He was forced to demonstrate the abilities of his sling once they were through the dangerous area, and in turn they let him examine their short spears and throwing sticks.

The hunters' village was another hour beyond that point and as Aaron approached he saw that it was larger than his own. There were also many more children of all ages in sight, and a quarter of the people were women. They did not live in tents as did Aaron's people, but in strange huts open to the air at ground level with mud-wattled thatched walls beginning at waist height and continuing up to a cone-shaped roof. Although the huts were no taller than Aaron's own tent they were at least three times that size in diameter.

There were also several stone structures, storehouses barred by heavy timbered doors, and rather than a single large field of grain the cultivated fields stretched away from the village on three sides. On the fourth, a small river was worked muddy below the village, the water supply taken from above by a bucket wheel. One further marvel was to catch his eye, for a log boat was on the river, dug out by fire, holding now a fisherman who was working with a net rather than a spear.

The hunters were seen as they approached the far edge of the fields, but they were halfway through the cultivated areas before the stranger amid them was noted. Most of the women and children were waiting for them as they came to the cleared circle in the center of the huts, but Aaron saw that there were few of the men. Then the village Elder was coming from his hut, the largest, and for a minute Aaron thought that he was seeing Joseph.

There were differences that showed instantly when the old man came closer, but his hair and his beard and even his demeanor were very like the old man who had guided Aaron's village for so many years. He was accompanied by two who were almost of his age, bearded as well, but it was clear that he was leader. They stopped short, facing the hunters from half a dozen paces away.

"You have returned with a stranger, Rik." The leader spoke slowly, his voice rasping. "Has there been a sending to you?"

"I am Aaron," he said, speaking for himself. "I come from my own people, in friendship."

"Aaron?" He coughed then and spat, and Aaron saw that there was blood with the phlegm. The old face was lined with pain and it was a minute before he could continue.

"There has been a sending," he said. "A very strange occurrence, unlike any sending I have ever seen. A new one is here, and he comes with a name on his tongue. There is much that is strange in this sending, signs, portents that to this moment I could not comprehend. But now the gods are making their message clear."

There was a disturbance then and a man ducked under

the wall of the largest hut; when he straightened he instantly caught the eyes of the returned hunters, and of Aaron. He was unlike any man ever seen in the world, for he was dressed from neck to foot in some strange glittering garment, night-black but shining in the day. Only his face and his hands showed clear, for even his feet were covered completely. There was the suggestion of Aaron's leather tunic in the garb but at the same time it was completely strange.

The oldster turned to the newcomer and it was obvious that he found it difficult to speak. He wiped his lips and indicated Aaron with his hand.

"This is he whose name you spoke," the old man said. "This is the one who calls himself Aaron."

The newcomer was staring, but Aaron could not read the expression on his face. "You said that he was not of your village," the man said harshly.

"I am Aaron," he said. "I am not of this village."

The newcomer was reaching against his clothes and then his hand disappeared, although Aaron could see no sign of a wallet. When his fingers reappeared he was holding something, his eyes going from it to Aaron's face.

"Aaron Caldwell?"

"I am Aaron," he repeated. "I know no person of the other name you have mentioned."

The newcomer was apparently satisfied. His hand disappeared again, then came out with something squat and black and ugly. He was holding out his hand toward Aaron, as though in friendship, and then there was a strange sound from the ugly thing, an ear-hurting noise that seemed strangely far away. In the same instant something powerful took hold of Aaron's heart and squeezed it, making him take a staggering step forward, one hand held out to the newcomer, eyes wide and mouth gaping as he gasped for breath. There was a bursting in his blood and in his eardrums, and then he was falling forward into the blackness of death. . . .

CHAPTER TEN

Martin lay tensed in the corner of a field. The moon was an hour above the horizon but the bulk of an urban tower several miles away was eating away at the edge of the disc. Stars spangled the cloudless sky but he could not sleep, listening constantly for noises that were alien to him: the chirrup of crickets, the nearly silent passage of a hunting owl, the movement of tiny animals through the hundred-yard swathe of underbrush that separated this field from its neighbor. Occasionally one of the small animals would try to cross the electronic barrier around the field and then there would be the crackle of ozone and the bleat of outrage and injury.

He shifted, trying to find a comfortable position, but he was not used to a hard surface beneath him when sleeping. The sleep-pac smoothed out most of the irregularities of the ground but the inch of gas-filled membrane was only an echo of the bed in his apartment. Even if by some miracle the bed had been transported to this field he would not have been able to sleep. Not since his Academy days had he been forced into such a situation and it displeased him to realize that life in the palace had so softened him.

He was a hundred miles from the city; the tower on the horizon was the last in this district, the lands surrounding the towers and stretching from here to the next district given over to the great automated farms that kept the citizens fed their basic allotment. He had moved through Old Town as quickly as possible after the warning, stopping only long enough to buy the sleep-pac and a packet of emergency rations with the money in his pockets. Solomon had long ago warned him to carry a generous supply of convertibles, for credit identification was worse than useless to a man on the run. The people of Old Town were not anxious to deal with him even on a cash basis, for ever since the raid on Solomon's house they had been in a full war against the hounds, the promise of long-tolerated sanctuary violated and forgotten. They would have dealt with one of their own no more kindly, and the man who outfitted him had urged him away with the same breath, lest his spoor paint a path straight to that house and mark its owner as collaborator and enemy of Lord Stennock's guardians.

The first strokes of silver dawn were just touching the edge of the sky when Martin gave up on the attempt to sleep. He rose quickly, collapsing the pac and stowing the slender envelope that contained it in a belt pocket. The stars had faded from the sky although the moon was still in the ascendancy, the great tower in the distance completely dark, sealed against the night and the world but for the red warning beacon circling on the communications tower at its peak.

There was a distant rumble, the clash of machinery as the farming robots came out of their subterranean caves, directed to begin the day's work even though sunrise was a good half hour away. Martin moved quickly to the barrier and jumped across it, the power level only a minor annoyance although repeated brushes could be fatal to the small animals that threatened the crops. Those who fell back after one sting, avoiding the barrier thereafter, were well enough off, however, for they served their purpose in the ecology. And the wild strips bordering the fields were seeded with food enough for the sustenance of the necessary level of wild population.

Martin moved cautiously through the woods, stopping once for fifteen minutes until the light level made it easier to see where he was going. The nearest road was half a mile away, across two intervening fields; he had been dropped at that point last night by a freighter whose services the underground had used in the past. Martin had met the carrier at the edge of Old Town, leaping aboard and later dropping off when it slowed so that the log of the computer would show no unusual or unexpected stops, thereby leading the driver to certain questioning by the lowest level of the Guard. The answers would be forced by drugs and fed inexorably on up the line to where someone of intelligence would eventually correlate them with other information and draw the logical conclusions.

There had been others before him in this stretch of borderland, the path faint to the untrained eye but obvious to those who knew what to look for: a narrow passage through thicket, a fallen log bridging an unexpected gully, a way of least resistance that enabled him to move almost as fast in the woods as he could in the open, once the sun had risen far enough to penetrate the umbrella of foliage. He followed the grid across two more fields before taking a turn to the north.

Here the woods widened measurably as the field was diminished by the natural course of a river. The water level was low, reduced along its headwaters by irrigation taps, but was still substantial; the land began to drop measurably now and a short way ahead Martin came out onto a precipice, the water slipping over to fall nearly a hundred feet to a rock-encircled natural pool. Where the river continued the near bank was along a fairly wide sand beach, white from this distance. But there was no obvious way down to that level, and now he had to pick his way with caution, coming to a place that was new to him.

"You may stop there."

He froze, then raised his hands before him and slowly looked around to see a shaggy-haired youngster holding a stun rifle on him. The weapon was guardian issue, but its holder was dressed in cutaway shorts and rubber-soled shoes, neither of which had ever seen the inside of a government plant.

"Solomon sends me," said Martin, backing up a step to more solid ground.

"The hounds have taken Solomon," the youth said.

"I know. They've had him under the probe, without success, and have him marked for the wipe."

"Who are you?"

"Ducas Martin of the royal household. Solomon and I have been exchanging services for a long time. Is Raselle here?"

The guard studied him for a moment without responding, then jerked his head. "Over here. There's a path."

At first Martin did not see it at all and then it was there, treacherous before him but a way down. But after he was on it he found that it was easier than it looked. Halfway down there was a narrow ledge, wide enough for three men to stand together if their backs were flat against the wall, and there the guard ordered him to stop.

There was still a fifty-foot drop before him, straight onto the rocks that surrounded the pool. The mist of the waterfall reached him, wetting his face, but the water was too fine to do more than touch gently against the artificial fibers of his clothes, not penetrating. He was looking straight at the river, following it through the little canyon until it disappeared from sight.

"In here."

He turned his head to see that an opening had appeared in the narrow space between the guard and himself. The hole was irregular and he could not see what had happened to the door. The gap was black against the bright morning, but as he stepped inside, hands out to guide him against the rough walls on either side, the darkness reddened slightly and he could see a few paces ahead.

"Watch your head."

He obeyed the warning and ducked low, walking low for perhaps twenty paces. The passage made a sudden turn to the left and then he was able to straighten again. Another turn three paces further, to the right, and the light level was slightly increased. Then a door was opened at the end of the passage—a wooden structure this time, in a frame cemented roughly to the opening; the walls here were built up with mortar—and he was in a broad natural cavern, perhaps a hundred feet long and half that in width, although the dimensions varied greatly. In places the ceiling was out of the reach of the light sources, while in others it came down low, to less than man-height.

The great room was filled with cartons of goods piled haphazardly in convenient corners, half a dozen tables and desks of variant description, the clutter of a barracks gathered all together in the one space. One section was set aside for dormitory and contained at least a dozen cots while another was set up as armory: there were three ranks of racked stun rifles similar to the one carried by the guard, and a host of other pieces both large and small.

Martin knew that this had been the source of the phony baby nuclear weapons Solomon had provided.

There was too much to take in all at once, for there was also activity: several men and women were busy at tasks that ranged from simple housekeeping—preparing a morning meal in the kitchen area—to the servicing of technical devices. Perhaps a third of the dormitory was occupied, and Martin recognized the silence generator that protected the sleepers against the outside activity.

Then his attention was caught by the ancient man behind the largest of the battered desk units. He lay stretched out full length in a recliner, hairless, skin chalk-white and stretched like parchment over the bones of the skull. The mouth was agape as he seemed to have difficulty breathing.

He looked toward Martin, touched a control at the side of his chair that slowly raised him into a normal sitting position. The guard prodded his prize forward, almost causing Martin to stumble; he half turned with a curse.

"We live in a climate of violence, Ducas Martin."

He stopped, looked back to the old man. The voice had been surprisingly strong, musically clear. Now as he stepped closer he saw that his first impression had been false: the man was not as old by a score of years as he had thought. The skin was tight-drawn but there was strength in the body and the sinewy flesh that had made him seem so thin.

"We have mutual friends, Ducas Martin," the man said now. "They warned us that you were coming. Lord Stennock is quite angry with his hounds for failing to find you."

"You are Raselle?" asked Martin, still uncertain.

"That is one of my names, yes. It will do as one which would interest the Prefect and his fellow criminals on the Council."

"You know me?"

"Yes," he said dryly. "I know you well. I am pleased that we finally have the opportunity to meet—I only wish that I could share this moment with the lady Karyn."

"You know the situation with Solomon?"

"Only that you have contacted him through I'bel da Canar. I know that he has been able to stand against the probe—else we would no longer be here."

Martin looked around the room. "Your people," he said. "Where did you recruit them? There have not been so many as this to escape the hounds. If you have this many here, then you must have an army in reserve elsewhere."

"We are an old organization," said Raselle. "Only part of our force comes from renegades. There are those here who are of the third generation in the struggle against the Empire."

"Impossible."

"We are patient," said Raselle. "We do not fight to free our own bodies from the chains for our souls are already free. If the whole world is to be with us then we must move with extreme caution."

"There are too many," said Martin. "How do you avoid the hounds, the probe? With this many you should all have been transported long ago."

"Some of us have been taken. But it has done Stennock and his predecessors little good, for our training is complete. We do not release a man into a position of danger until we are certain that he can stand against the probe. And of course we have few who know anything beyond that necessary to their own tasks. What value to the probe a cipher who knows nothing beyond his own conviction that the hounds are hateful, the Empire evil?"

He stood up and leaned across the desk to activate a

projection of the planet, spinning ever on its axis, oblivious to the activities of the tiny parasites clinging to its surface crust. "There is our army, Ducas Martin—the citizens of Earth. In time they will rise in answer to our call and cast off the shackles of the Empire."

"Pretty words, but empty. Nothing can stir the citizens into action."

"It will be difficult," Raselle admitted. "But once they do begin to move, then beware, my friend, for nothing can stand against them."

"Perhaps . . . someday. But now is when we must help Solomon."

"You are right, the time for revolution has not yet come. But I fear there is little we can do for our overweight friend—we cannot penetrate the defenses of the hounds. No, Solomon will be transported."

"That's exactly what we want," said Martin.

Raselle blinked. "You can explain?"

"If you can act."

The palace gardens always attracted a large percentage of the upperclass, and even a few bold midclass workers who had noticed that the guardians never bothered to clear them away. This was supposed to be a public part of the palace, open to everyone from citizen rank up. Thus the several merchant-robed men who passed singly into the cool walks over the space of half an hour drew no special attention from the monitors on duty. It was rare that anything exciting happened here, years since there had been a demonstration requiring the use of guardians.

Martin was the third to enter, the others preceding in the event that his disguise were penetrated at some station along their route. But there were no more than the normal number of guardians in the streets and he managed to enter the city through one of the freight transport stations without trouble.

He stopped in the undercity long enough to attempt contact with the garish man but could not reach him; nor could the message drop say when he would return. There was fear in the man's eyes although he dared not ask Martin to leave—the ability of the underground to respond was as feared as the powers of the hounds.

The streets of the undercity seemed lighter of traffic than usual and those who were there told their purpose in their garb—technies on repair call, servant lackeys hurrying to their duties, service ranks of every kind. But there were few of the guardians visible, far fewer than normal; Martin wondered if they had been dispatched to other duty.

Whatever, something had served to clear the pleasure seekers from their usual haunts. He passed a number of twenty-four-hour pleasure stations and found that every third one was closed. He assigned one of Raselle's men to determine if it was only lack of business or if there was some more sinister force behind the disruptions.

The man returned an hour later to report that he had been unable to reach the normal underground contacts in Old Town. A pall seemed to have dropped over the entire district, the denizens retreating behind the hoped-for safety of locked doors. If the night life had been diminished in the at least lawful sections of the undercity, there beyond the law it was extinguished entirely. But there had been advance word at Raselle's headquarters that things were troubled in Old Town and so they had not attempted to return by that path.

There was one more call that he wanted to make but

he dared not contact the hospital where Tomas had been taken. And here even Raselle's widespread network could not help him no matter how anxious he was for news of the boy. There had never been reason for them to plant someone in that place, normally only a recovery station for members of the Guard and their families, and there was no time to attempt such a penetration now. He received sympathy but no more from the several oblique sources he tried to use, leaving him to worry about the boy as a distraction from his other problems.

After an hour he reached the gardens and slipped in without attracting attention. The palace had been a center of Empire intrigue since the very time of its construction and the guardians were not the only ones with secrets that did not appear on the published plans. Karyn possessed a few private resources of her own, one a lift that operated from the garden level directly to her own apartment. In years past she had used it as a means of slipping out with Martin to taste the joys of the undercity.

Now he made certain that the men he had assigned to guard duty against the guardians were in their positions and surveying the monitors, then he took one man with him to the secret entrance.

The tiny lift discharged them in Karyn's private chambers, secluded even from the normal serving staff, and here they were forced to wait for nearly an hour. When the Empress appeared, breathless, anxiety lined her face until she was certain that it was Martin.

Then she exploded. "Four days! Where have you been? There is a Council order against you—a final order, authorizing full precautions even to death!"

Martin was stunned by the news. The step was unheard of, for the government was benevolent even when at its most tyrannical. Thus the development of the mind wipe and the transportation of those considered incorrigible. It was obviously the work of Lord Stennock, but it could have been approved only by the full Council in conference.

"Stennock is scared," he said.

"Stennock is furious," said Karyn. "He came here, to my rooms, last night—forced his way in. He as much as accused me of treason."

"What news from I'bel?"

"None for two days. She has been with the wipe for that entire time. But when I last spoke with her she said Solomon was still standing against the probe."

"He won't crack."

"I pray you're right, Ducas. I'bel is prepared to subvert the wipe as I ordered. I had to renew the pressure against her, though. I hope she has the strength to stand through all."

Martin closed his eyes, pressing his fingers against his temples to massage away a sudden pain. "She may be the weakest link. But I think Stennock has no reason to suspect her involvement. There is still much that has to be done, however, people to be contacted. For some of them the word will have to come from you—men who are still loyal to you." He did not add that those he would see today owed their first loyalty to Raselle, and against the Empire and its representatives.

There were a number of surprised men who received an invitation to call upon their Empress that very day and at their earliest convenience. The messages were delivered through a number of devious routes that bypassed normal channels of palace information to avoid rousing the suspicion of the guardians. Wherever possible the recipients were ordered to safe stations, but a few had to come directly to the palace.

Most of those contacted today were deep agents, long buried against the time of most urgent need—there were a few who had been subservient to the ruling system for so long that they had forgotten youthful dreams of revolution. Raselle's man was empath enough to detect such uncertainties—too many, more than they had anticipated —and their force was depleted by the forced assignment of some of their own people to guard duty over the waverers.

There was also difficulty in persuading certain of the others that Martin was bona fide, for his position in the palace was too well known and they were not yet ready to accept the idea of the Empress as a fellow traveler. Then Martin was forced to expend his energy in convincing others of the sure men that death was not the easy answer to their problems with individuals. It was mostly the younger men that Raselle had sent who reacted that way, those who had grown up in the underground, receiving their orientation from their parents and not from their peers. Those born within the system had been indoctrinated since birth and through all further programming to the theory of nonviolence.

It was midnight before the last of the contacts had been made, leaving Martin drained of energy. Although his own role in the proceedings to come would be major, the final course to success or failure had already been determined and was out of his hands. If Raselle was right in the choice of his agents, and they in turn were as capable as they were supposed to be, then they would win.

He had left the palace three times during the course of the day, each time the danger of apprehension increasing. As night approached even though the actual fact of darkness could never be noticed in the perpetual-day world that was the undercity, the number of guardians in the street increased steadily.

"They suspect the night," said Raselle's man. "It's the traditional time for the criminal, illicit activity. A final coup, if it is ever to succeed, will have to be planned for high noon."

———————◆———————

Martin waited an hour before turning to the palace, dismissing the other man before he approached the great public entrance. He had removed his masquerade except for a sheltering cowl, and now he stripped that away and stepped clearly through the barrier and into the arms of the waiting hounds. They came up to him before he had taken a dozen steps across the lobby and froze him with a quick stun, handling him roughly in the process. Muscles locked and eyes frozen to what was straight ahead, he was aware that he was being handled like a piece of baggage, trundled onto a cart and carried swiftly to the lifts. He could not tell what level they stopped at nor who was with them, but when the antidote was broken beneath his nose he shook his head to clear it of the fumes. He worked the tension from back muscles and saw that he was in an office with the Prefect of Police.

"There is such a thing as courtesy," he said, still uncomfortable from the effects of the freezer. "If they had asked I would have come."

"There has been a warrant out for you for four days," said the Prefect, visibly angry. He seemed to be controlling an explosion with the greatest difficulty. "Where have you been?"

Martin shrugged. "Here."

"Here in the palace?"

"In the city."

Stennock stared for a moment, jaw quivering. "I suppose you would say that you were on the business of the Empress."

"That is where I serve."

Stennock sat down behind the desk. The office was obviously borrowed, for the furniture was not to his scale; he filled the chair completely, leaving no room for anything but his bulk.

"You act the fool, Ducas Martin," he said then. "You are a talented man but your talents have brought you nothing but the most serious trouble. Perhaps you think you've been playing a game?"

"I leave games for the spoiled, m'lord," he replied.

Stennock stared at him a moment longer without speaking, then the door opened in response to a signal Martin had not seen him give, admitting two guardians. The Prefect snapped his hand as though in disgust.

"Take him away."

Then he turned in his chair to stare at the false image until they were gone.

Martin was taken to another room on the same level, one obviously intended to be a detention cell. He was permitted to walk this time, a guard at either shoulder and two more following. One unlocked the toilet facilities of the room and two of them stood over him as he used them; then they were relocked. The one guard sat down on the only chair in the room, leaving him the single bunk that had already been folded down; the others left, locking the door behind them.

He reached into his pocket and found that they had emptied them during the moments of stasis. He had nothing left, not even a handkerchief. He looked around the room, quickly noting the details of the two doors and the two single pieces of furniture, then gave up and lay down on the bunk. Within minutes he was asleep; it had been a long day and he did not know when the hounds would leave him such a chance for rest again.

The hand on his shoulder was insistent rather than rough. He opened his eyes, blinking, but it was perhaps ten seconds before he oriented himself. Then he was sitting up, rubbing the back of his head.

The same guard was still in the room but another had entered; there was the business of unlocking the toilet now, the two standing so close as to be embarrassing. He wet his finger and tried to scrub his teeth, then swallowed a handful of water, which reminded his stomach that it was empty. They had taken his watch so he had no way of determining the time but to his inner clock it felt late.

They did not intend to feed him, however; he was hurried to a lift and then high into the tower, and when he stepped out he saw that he was on the Council floor. The half-moon table was there three steps above him, the high-backed chairs marked with the symbol of their occupant empty now. Lord Stennock's was on the end, to Martin's left as he faced the chamber, the symbol the circle of peace crossed by the sword of justice.

He was in the dock but the chair usually there for witnesses and petitioners to the Council was gone, forcing him to stand. The gallery above was empty, sign that the meeting was closed, although there was an unusual number of guardians present even for such an occasion.

And now the Council was coming into the chamber by twos and threes, filing into their places, whispering among themselves. Stennock appeared briefly, gave an order, then the royal box was opened. Martin stared in surprise, for Karyn was invited to the Council only on the most public of state occasions, when nothing was ever presented for discussion or decision. But a moment later she came in, pausing at the rail to look down at Martin —the only occupant of the high levels to do so; the members of the Council seemed agreed to ignoring him. She sat down quickly, Martin unable to read the expression on her face.

Then Stennock returned and took his place and the others slowly settled down. Lexalt, the aged Council Chairman, stood after another moment of conference with his neighbor, Blume of Communications, holding a sheet of paper. He seemed to be regarding it with dismay and even embarrassment but he managed to speak.

"M'lady"—he bowed to Karyn—"m'lords, we have been asked to assemble together in plenary conference to receive news and charges of the gravest import." His voice was high-pitched, unpleasant to the ear, and he trembled as he spoke. He was as broad as Stennock but inches shorter, his bulk coming almost entirely from fat. "This conference has been sealed according to the wishes of one of our members, as concurred by a majority of the Council. Rather than attempt a translation of the charges, I will hand this proceeding over to Lord Stennock."

Stennock did not bother to rise. He inclined his head sardonically to the royal box: "M'lady," and then toward his fellows: "M'lords. I thank you for your indulgence. The matter at hand is most serious, for it involves complicity in the highest crimes and at the very highest levels of the Empire." Did he look again to Karyn? His next words proved that he had. "Indeed, it is only with the greatest of pain that I as a most loyal subject say this, but the truth is that there has been misprision at the very throne!"

The charge was unfamiliar to Martin but the Council understood. And he knew by their grim visages that the charge had not come as a surprise.

"Yes, m'lords, there has been misprision—treason—by the very throne, aided in and abetted by this man who stands before us, this one who calls himself Ducas Martin rather than by the honest citizen's name that was given to him at birth. It has not been their intent to subvert and circumvent this Council, no—it has been their aim to destroy the very Empire!"

He looked at Martin for the first time. "The charges are documented in the reports that you received. There is no question as to the penalty for the accomplice—I have already ordered the mind wipe prepared, and he will be transported by the first available ship. But what are we to do with this other person, m'lords? What are we to do with our Karyn, our Empress?"

Now protests came from several of the others. "See here, Stennock!" It was Kadel of Transport. "We owe respect to the throne no matter what its present occupant may or may not have done!"

"I stand rebuked, m'lord." He inclined his head. "We do owe our respect to the Empress—but that is all! Any vow of allegiance that we have made in the past has been thrown back in our teeth. There are among us a few who think the lady Karyn herself should be transported"—he held up his hands to cut off the renewal of protest—"but I do not agree that so drastic a measure is necessary. We will have to place certain controls over the allowable activities, of course, but I think we can solve the problem that easily. It is the lady's companions who have led her to this state, and that we will not have to worry about any further."

CHAPTER ELEVEN

As Aaron stared at the newcomer his newfound sensitivity touched the evil in the man's mind, saw the terrible thing that would happen to his body. Even before the finger could tighten against the stud he was falling forward, aware that he must pretend to the harm that the other willed him. The movements came so closely together that the man did not realize he had narrowly missed, that only Aaron's left arm had taken the sting of the beam. Now that elbow hurt strangely, as though the joint had been pulled away from him. He could not recognize the touch of ice, for this world never grew that cold below the polar latitudes.

The actions of the newcomer astonished everyone, but as Aaron fell forward they reacted in the same instant. Before the man could bring up his gun again the hunters who had returned with Aaron were on him, twisting back his arm, kicking out his legs from beneath him. He fell heavily and saw the stunner go skittering away, and then there was the point of a spear at his throat.

"Apes!" The man spat after using the unfamiliar word, but they recognized it as insult. He was looking straight into the sky rather than at their faces, and his struggles were done.

Aaron got clumsily to his feet, holding his left arm. For a moment it was as though the lower arm had been chopped away, although as he looked at his hand and thought about it he could see the fingers wiggle. The numbness was spreading into his shoulder now, but with it was needle pain.

"Are you all right?" asked the Elder anxiously, ashamed that this terrible insult should have happened in his village.

Aaron swallowed, then drew a tentative deep breath as he released his arm. Sensation was already returning to it in a rush of jabbing heat as he flexed his shoulder. He rubbed his shoulder gingerly.

"I am all right," he said. "But this . . . who is he? Where does he come from?"

The man laughed and looked at Aaron now. "Don't you know me . . . *son?* I am one of your gods."

The old man stiffened, then moved away from the man on the ground. His eyes were frightened as he shook his head. "No!" he said softly. "That cannot be!"

The man laughed again, harder now, until he was suddenly in a paroxysm of strangling mirth that nearly doubled him over. His eyes were filled with tears and his hand beat lightly against the ground as he shook his head. The man holding the spear moved back a step, as though the madness could contaminate him, but even as he acted the spell was ending. The stranger choked on his laughter, and then on bile, leaning over and raising his head a few inches to be sick. Then he sat up, keeping a wary eye on the spear holder. He wiped his face, then slowly got to his feet.

"You thought the gods brought me," he said, confronting the old man. "You thought they sent me! Sweet merciful heaven, what a joke! All these years you people thought that we were gods—what a stupid, pointless joke! You've never known that you were condemned to be here!"

———————◆———————

Martin was hurried from the Council level even before Karyn was given permission to leave her box. He did not see the guardians who accompanied her now, for he was unconscious as soon as he was through the door. His handlers dragged him unceremoniously across the room, treating him far more roughly than was either necessary or normal. The word had come down to the guardians that this one was to receive no special favors, no matter his former position in the palace; and there were always those to interpret such a lack of instruction in the manner most personally satisfying.

He came awake to find himself in a hospital bed, his clothing gone, his body sore in a dozen unexpected places. Even his personal jewelry had been taken this time, leaving him nothing but a pair of issue pajamas. He raised his hand to his right earlobe, which felt curiously light, fingering the place where an antique band of gold normally dangled. Many years ago it had been one of the first truly personal gifts from the young Empress to the man who was becoming her most trusted aide and he had worn it ever since.

He let his eyes close again for a moment as he tried to localize the various areas of pain. Then he opened them to see a guard seated across the way, by the door, and then another bed a few paces away from his own. It was in use, but he could not make out the occupant. He raised his hand again, then let it drop heavily to the bed, the faint sound catching the attention of the guard. He touched a call signal and a moment later the door opened to admit first an aging nurse and then, seconds later, Lord Stennock.

"Only one guard?" Martin asked.

Stennock smiled. "You still have a sense of humor. Even that one is unnecessary, for no one has ever escaped from this place. You know of course that you are about to undergo the wipe, and then transportation."

He said nothing, and after a moment, when the nurse was finished with her fussing, the Prefect moved around the bed to where he could indicate the other person in the room.

"Have you met your roommate, Martin? I think it's someone whose company you'll enjoy."

He touched the control and the bed began to elevate, bringing Tomas into Martin's view. The boy was either asleep or unconscious.

"Your barracks brat. Since you were so interested in his welfare I thought it appropriate to let him accompany you to your new home. Of course, once you've been through the wipe—and I may let you take that together, too—neither of you will remember the other. But I'm sure you'll make friends again quickly enough." Then he laughed. "If I don't order you dropped on opposite sides of the planet, that is."

Martin knew that he was being baited although he was not sure of Stennock's motives. But he was glad to see Tomas, even in this situation. If he was able to save himself then he could certainly save the boy as well.

"No probe?" he asked then. The Prefect's eyes narrowed just enough for him to notice, and then he was smiling again.

"We're all done with that business, Martin. You've spilled your pretty little insides all over the place. We've managed to clean out the lot of your country friends—including Raselle."

He knew that the Prefect was lying although he did not

know why. But he knew enough of the probe to know that anyone who had been ripped apart by it would remember the terrible pain, the trauma of losing their most precious store of memories to the cold handling of others.

"Enjoy your last hours with the brat," said Stennock then. "You're scheduled to be wiped in"—he glanced at his watch—"exactly two hours. I'll see you there—this is one that I would not let myself miss."

The time passed far more quickly than Martin would have wanted. After Stennock left he managed to sit up on the edge of his bed, although his legs did not hold strength enough to help him down and over to Tomas's side. He could only watch the boy from here, hoping for some sign that he was aware of what had been happening, what was going to happen. But Tomas remained in his unconscious state and after a time Martin began to suspect that he was drugged, as one last torment for the man.

The door opened to admit the nurse and a physician, and behind them I'bel da Canar. She waited until Martin was sedated, then moved beside his bed, staring down with eyes devoid of emotion. She had made no indication that she knew him, offered him no sign that he was not to worry. But for the sake of his sanity he had to think that everything was proceeding according to the plan he had so carefully worked out with Karyn.

He was losing all sensation in his body as the bed was wheeled from the room, unable to turn his head to see if Tomas was coming too. If he closed his eyes there was nothing; he was completely divorced from his body, afloat in the blackness of space. There were not even the scatterings of false color normally seen by the brain against the screen of the eyelids.

He opened his eyes again, conscious that equipment

was being moved into position around him. Something passed across his vision, too close to be made out, and he knew that electrodes were being attached to his skull even though he could not actually feel them; it was as though everything were being done to another.

Then his eyes were being closed for him by heavy weights, and he lost everything. . . .

———◆———

Three days passed before Aaron came into territory that was familiar to him. He was astonished at the distance he had covered, and wondered how many hours the mad flight had lasted. Could it have been more than a single day? Never before that had he driven his body to the point of absolute exhaustion, and although there was no memory of day blending into night and then into day again, he could think of no other explanation for the impossible amount of ground—unless at some point he had taken flight with the wind dreamers.

There were five in the party now—the hunter Rik and the boy, Rik's son, and another hunter from their village who called himself Holt. And the stranger was with them too, the man who claimed to have come from the sky. The god, if such he were, was weaker than mortal men; he had early protested at the pace set by the others, forcing them to hang back and stop for frequent rests.

Before freeing the other from the bonds that had kept him their prisoner in the village Aaron carefully went through his pockets and then the rest of his garments. He removed everything, finding little that made sense; but he had claimed two things for himself—the fire maker and a marvelously contrived knife that was sharper by far than any stone implement. The other things, unintelligible to them, had been left in the care of Rik's Elder.

Despite the circumstances the sky man seemed strangely amused, and now that Aaron said that they were approaching his village, even light-hearted. But he would not tell the joke, even though he had taken to whistling a little melody to himself. The strangeness of his actions made Aaron cautious and his caution was rewarded when he stopped twenty minutes away from the village, telling the others to remain while he scouted ahead.

He stopped just out of sight of the village. The fields he had passed were deserted although the grain was approaching the time of ripening. Moving silently into the woods, he let his mind open and almost immediately it impinged upon the presence of a sky master.

. . . *man-creature?* . . .

Yes, free one!

And then there was a second, and a third, and through them he was suddenly aware that his probing thoughts were darting around the world, from wind dreamer to dreamer. There was the impression of the great globe of the planet wheeling beneath him, turning and tumbling as he was in first one set of eyes and then another. There was the great desert made tiny, the smear of a giant hand wiping across the continent; and all around that the tang of roaring white surf as the world ocean pounded against the upstart land intrusions. He was so high that he could see the curve of the planet, and then moving low, majestically slow, over a range of wooded mountains and hills that housed the new little two-legged creatures—

—and he knew that he was seeing his own village, and now he was back in his own mind, brain suddenly assaulted by odors and sounds and tastes that was only the normal world registering in a normal way. But after the touch of the sky masters it seemed very different, alien to the proper way of life.

The winds are troubled . . .

He knew that it was the one he had contacted first, although there was nothing that a man's mind could mark as identification in that touch.

The gods have come down to men, formed Aaron.

. . . there are no gods; there is only God. Those who would be are false . . .

There are more from the sky?

. . . not from the sky, but beyond, from a place that even we cannot reach. There are many—there. They are like you, but they are not you. . . .

Aaron sent the touch of his mind out toward the village, toward his own kind, and he was rewarded with a dozen, twice dozen, responses in return. Most of them he recognized—James the carper, struck now to his bed by the failure of his body, ever complaining; the woman Aryll, who had shared Aaron's bed on lonely occasions; Rob, sore worried as he tried to put away the staff of authority. But there was one that was different, strange, new; yet like that mind that had signaled hatred for him though never knowing him. The sky men had come here, too. . . .

When Martin recovered consciousness he knew instantly that he was in space. He lay quietly for a moment, not opening his eyes, feeling the intangible vibrations in his mind that came from the drive generators. His awareness was total in the instant of awakening and with it came a deep feeling of triumph: his mind was still his own.

He opened his eyes to see that he was in a dormitory,

in the middle bunk of a tier of three. He turned his head and counted half a dozen more stackings in that direction, and then found three more to the other side. There was another row immediately across from him.

There were others; perhaps half the bunks were occupied. But there was no sign of the guardians. He sat up quickly, slipped out of the bunk, then stood for a moment on shaky knees. The dormitory had originally been a cargo hold, by its high ceiling; the amenities were simple, the toilet arrangements in the open in the far corner. There were two women among the bodies he could see —one was the lady Dianne, who was there with several of the others from the aborted uprising. All were naked, and there was no place for clothing lockers.

Martin made his way along the beds, finding Solomon against the near wall. The fat man came instantly awake when he touched his shoulder, staring at Martin for several seconds. Then he grinned and swung his bulk up to where he could slam Martin's shoulder.

"We did it!" he said. "The lady I'bel came through."

Martin held up his hand for silence, then formed words with his lips. "How many of us? We may be the only ones to have escaped the wipe."

Solomon nodded his understanding, then watched as he continued searching the tiers until he found Tomas. The boy's skin was cold to his touch and he was slow to respond. Then his eyes were open—and staring blankly.

"Tomas!" Martin's fists clenched. "Do you know me?"

There was no response. After a minute the boy moved his head to take in the bunks next to him and then his eyes closed and he was asleep.

Martin started to reach for his shoulder again, then stopped. The sense of loss was terrible—but he had known from the moment in Solomon's house that Tomas was lost to him. It was enough now that the boy was alive; he would make up for the other things done to him.

Others were coming awake now, disturbed from their slumber by his prowling. He stopped by several he recognized, but the response was the same as from Tomas: blankness. A few were sitting up, responding to natural functions, but most seemed to want nothing more than to return to sleep.

He made his way back to Solomon, angry. "They're like sheep! Why don't they soil themselves?"

"They've had intensive deep hypnotic retraining," said Solomon. "They can be dropped onto the transport world and they will have the basic skills needed to survive. That, and a name."

"But they aren't even alive!"

"They live," said Solomon softly, not reminding the other that he had sent many of them to this fate. "They will be able to rebuild their lives. The only question we cannot answer—is it tragedy? or blessing?"

During the next two hours Martin examined the dormitory. There was only one door and that locked from the other side. He was sure that they were being monitored but there was no communications equipment that he could use to contact the control center of the ship. The bunks were welded in place and the mattress material fastened so tightly to the metal that Martin could not break the bond, although he kept trying. Even the water taps and exchangers were protected by strong guards, use sensitive, the taps flowing only when someone was within six inches, closing when they backed away.

An alarm rang and all around them sleepers were waking and clambering down from their beds. The wiped ones ignored each other, managing somehow to avoid touching one another. When the alarm rang again a panel opened in the wall, disgorging rations. The transportees shuffled to the rack, in no particular order but without pushing or fighting. Each managed to get a ration, which they took back to their bunks.

Sudden awareness of an empty place in his belly made Martin get to the rack just in time to grab the last two packets away from an early finisher who turned away disappointed but not argumentative. He took the packages back to Solomon, who made a face.

"Pap," the fat man said. The food was a single cake, compressed tightly and moist enough to be palatable, but there was no strong taste. "Fortified with all the essentials for life put in, and all the flavor taken out. Garbage!"

"Eat it," said Martin, who had been chewing without thinking. "Husband your energy."

"I'd rather live on my fat," said Solomon. But he ate.

Hours passed, to become a day and then days, a succession of alarms signaling the human cattle into activity although the light level never changed, never varied. Meals arrived every twelve hours, and midway through the "day" period the transportees would roll out to shamble about the limited space for a period of fifteen minutes. The exercise kept their muscles from turning flaccid, for between times they kept to their bunks, content to pass their hours in sleeping. If the hold was monitored and notice taken of Martin and Solomon as deviates from the routine nothing was ever done about it; no guards appeared.

They had no way of knowing how long they had been on the ship before the first awakening—it might have been the first day or the hundredth—but after that time twenty days had passed. Martin set up a routine of exercise that kept him in tone and served to alleviate an hour of boredom. At each session Solomon watched his exertions with amusement, refusing to join in. After the eighth day he began to deliberately exhaust himself, the boredom of the routine and the never-changing time more than he could stand. He had taken by then to snapping waspishly at Solomon, for the fat man had a trick of losing himself for hours in a contemplation that Martin could not share. But the other would not rise to the argument that he was trying to force, always returning intended insult with a smile.

The change came on the twentieth day, during the hours Martin had taken to calling "night." He came instantly awake, knowing that something was wrong. The transportees were still asleep but Solomon had also come awake and was sitting up on the edge of his bunk, hand raised to warn Martin to silence as he listened intently. But there was nothing to hear.

Then he knew: the drive generators had ceased their constant manipulation of the atoms and subatomic particles that made up the ship and everything within its space.

The ship had stopped.

Twenty minutes later the door opened.

Aaron cautiously circled the village, slipping unseen behind the main cluster of tents, taking cover behind a pile of uncured hides that were stinking in the sun. Flies rose in fright as he came close, then circled wildly for a moment before settling back. He had not noticed them before but now he was aware that the image of the entire village was slovenly. In the old place this would never have been permitted to happen, but the people had too much here, far more than they could use. And the bad habits were showing every place.

Most of the men of the village were gathered before Aaron's tent—Rob's now, he realized, for Rob had done as he had suggested and taken the seat of power. The sky man was with them, seated at Rob's side above the others. He seemed a little younger than his fellow, although it was difficult to tell as both had shaved their heads. His garments were of the same night-shining material as the other wore—could have been the very same pieces, except that Aaron knew that the other man still held his.

Aaron had discussed the courses of possible action with Rik and Holt, should it be that the sky men had come to every village looking for him. Now his hand dug for his sling and brought out with it a small pebble; he wanted only to stun the man, not kill him. Just as the sky man rose to his feet, by chance looking in his very direction, Aaron was standing and letting the stone fly straight to its target, a burst of pent-up anger exploding at the same instant. The man let out a roar of pain, grabbing his forehead; then he was fumbling for the twin of the other's pain-maker.

Aaron had misjudged the weight of the stone. Now he quickly grabbed another, larger this time, and was whirling the sling even before the man had his gun from his belt. This time the other dropped unconscious.

The villagers were stunned, several of the men half risen, both by Aaron's surprising appearance and by his attack on the sky man. They cried out now as he ran to the man, bent quickly to strip him of the sky things. Then he was standing, looking about to find thongs hanging on the flap of the tent. He took them and used them to secure the man's hands and legs.

Questions, demands, were exploding from Rob and the bolder men of the village. Aaron shook his head, refusing to explain, waiting until the babble had ceased.

. . . quick done, man-creature . . .

The contact surprised him. *Did I do right?*

. . . you have begun . . .

The touch was gone but there was satisfaction in the thought. He looked up, as though he could see the creature who had formed it, but the sky was empty of everything but small clouds. Even the lesser creatures of the air seemed stilled, silent, as though they understood what had passed among them and were in awe.

He gave orders, no one objecting to his resumption of the position of leadership. Even Rob seemed glad that he had returned to handle this new situation. Setting two men to watch the sky man, he took Rob with him to go out to meet Rik and his fellows. There was an awkward moment, Rob astonished now too many times in succession to be able to accept the constant casting over of the routine of life.

They brought the sky men together again, the first stopping in surprise as he saw his trussed counterpart.

"They got you, eh?"

There was a swelling on the man's temple; he stared at Aaron, recognizing his leadership. "Are you the one who took me?"

Aaron nodded. "Why do you we once thought gods fear me so? The hatred will burst your gut, poison your blood."

"We don't hate you," said the first.

"You would do me harm!"

He shrugged, looked to the other. "It is our job—our assigned place."

"Someone must hold the hatred," Aaron insisted. "It spills through your eyes, your tongue."

The man was embarrassed. "We underestimated you."

"We had no way of knowing," said the other, speaking

to his fellow in self-defense. Then he was struggling to a more comfortable position. "Can I be untied? I think you've cut off the circulation in my hands."

Aaron nodded and he was released, then helped to his feet by the other. As they stood together the resemblance was even more remarkable.

"Sergeant Major will be displeased," said the second sky man. "I wonder what nastiness he'll contrive for this failure."

The first looked to Aaron. "There are others of us, you know—we dropped a man at every tribal outposting on the planet, wherever we could find life force indicating the presence of an adult male. They'll be coming after us."

Aaron looked to the sky. "Your people are powerful—but there are other powers. I am not helpless."

"You think you can stand against the Empire?"

"I know not your Empire—whether it be terrible weapon or the force of great numbers. But I fear it not. If it is intended for me to stand against Empire then I shall stand. If the gods . . . God . . . have decreed failure, then I shall fail. Whichever, I shall do what must be done, meet what must be."

The first two through the door were guardians, one with an officer's pips at his collar. Then Martin saw that they were shackled and relaxed as they were herded into the dormitory by two of the ship's company. They were followed by the commander—one of the men Karyn had summoned to the palace.

"You could have come in sooner," said Martin.

"I didn't want to arouse their suspicion," said the commander. "I am not certain enough that the whole crew is loyal to me and the Empress."

One of the men carried coversuits, which he gave to Martin and Solomon. The fat man's was large but he was barely able to seal the seams. The feeling of clothes was strange for a few minutes to Martin, after having gone naked so long. But there was a dignity that came with the suits and he quickly readjusted.

"We've reached rendezvous with the royal yacht," the commander said then. "We should make contact within the hour."

He turned to one of his men and ordered the guardians to be unshackled. Martin protested.

"What about the others?"

"There are only the two. What need of guardians for these sheep?"

Martin glanced around the hold and saw that the interruption had drawn no attention from the transportees. Most of them were still sleeping.

He went then to Tomas, touched the boy to bring him out of his sleep. The eyes opened, staring at him, but there was still no sign of recognition, nor even of intelligence. He saw only a blankness, a lack, that stabbed deep into his gut, churning his feelings. He closed his eyes for a brief moment, then turned away before opening them again, refusing to look at the boy again.

The commander took them to the ship's lounge, left them in the care of a steward who did the best he could with military stores to come up with a decent meal, a fine wine. Solomon expressed his satisfaction although the tightness of his suit hindered him from full charge through the plates. Martin ate listlessly, however, not tasting what he did swallow; it might all have been transportee rations.

The ship was old, converted from express duty to transportee service when it should have been scrapped. It was comfortable enough and the Third Officer did his best to keep them company, but Martin was relieved when the bridge announced on the intercom that the royal yacht had just broken out of drive. A few minutes later there was a loud clunk as the two ships made contact, and then the Empress was being escorted into the lounge.

"Ducas?" She stopped at seeing him, as though not sure until this minute that he was all right.

He inclined his head. "M'lady." Then she was holding him, kissing him, overwhelming him with the violence of her relief, her welcome.

"You bloody fool! I was so worried, even when I'bel said that everything had gone according to plan. God, how I've worried!"

He moved his head back and smiled. "You do have feelings for me, m'lady?"

"Damn you, Ducas Martin! You know I love you!"

The others in the lounge backed from the hatch, pretended to be deeply occupied, until at last Martin moved away from Karyn to see that I'bel de Canar had come with her on the yacht. He stared.

"A refugee, lady I'bel? Or volunteer?"

"Both," she said sadly. "I confessed to our Empress that I found it difficult to serve the wipe any longer—or stay in Lord Stennock's service, having put him through his own machine."

"Stennock wiped?" He stared again, in disbelief.

"It was foolish of me," she said. "A whim."

"I'bel protests too much," said Karyn. "She did it to save me from the probe."

"He wouldn't dare!"

"He did dare," she said flatly. "Lord Stennock thought that he could convince the Council to accept him as consort. I was not asked."

"It seemed an easy way out of the situation," said I'bel. "The throne would be preserved, the Empress's image saved. I'm afraid our rash actions left matters in a good deal of confusion—there have been several changes on the Council already, the chairs Stennock supported collapsing."

"I have approved most of the changes," said Karyn. "As is my right as Empress . . . my undisputed right, now."

"Our people . . . ?" he asked.

"The hounds are under a new leash," said I'bel. "A man called Raselle."

A long sigh of relief escaped his lips. He looked at the commander of the ship. "How far to the transport planet?"

"Another short jump, then three days at sublight."

"What are the arrangements there?"

"There's a cadre of forty-four on the permanent station. Most of them are new, we rotated them in last trip. The station takes care of the actual transfer to the surface."

"Then they would know Aaron Caldwell's position?"

"I doubt it," he said, shrugging. "I don't think they keep that close a watch over the individuals. There's never been a retrieval that I know of."

"How many groups are on the surface?"

The commander shrugged again. "The last census counted ten thousand individuals—perhaps two hundred, three hundred separate groups. Of course, life spans are fairly short—something like twelve surface years after transport. I understand Caldwell was transported twenty years ago. The odds are against his still being alive."

Martin looked at Karyn. "He's alive. He has to be alive."

CHAPTER TWELVE

The last jump to the sun of the transport world was done quickly, in a matter of minutes, but the three-day fall toward the planet itself was an eternity long, tedious at every moment. They were so close now to the goal toward which they had been working that neither Martin nor Karyn could satisfy themselves with sitting patiently.

They were in the lounge now, watching the simulation of the sun in the view screen. It had grown visibly larger although the planet was still only a glowing green dot to the lower left.

Martin worked at his lower lip. "How long will it take to reverse the wipe?"

I'bel stared at him, shocked. "You can't reverse the wipe," she said after a moment. "The process is total."

He stared in return. "Then how do we restore Aaron Caldwell?"

"You can't 'restore' him," she said. "You can reeducate him, using as accurate a reconstruction of his early life as you can obtain. Of course, it's terribly expensive—you need actors, sets, a record of experiences. I wish there were a way to make a complete recording of the mind as it was being wiped, because we would only have to play it back. But that isn't possible."

"How long does it take to reeducate them?" he asked then.

I'bel shrugged. "How long does it take a child to become an adult? Years. Oh, not a lifetime—he is an adult now, and he has many years of other experiences to draw upon. But he will have to relearn what he once was, everything that he once did. If he had technical training, he will have to go through the entire course again."

"You still are talking of years," said Martin.

She nodded. "Yes. At least several. How long really depends a great deal on the subject."

"Will he be whole when you finish?"

"Of course not—perhaps," she said, changing her mind. "I don't know. I can't say—no one knows. There have only been one or two reconstructions, and they were deliberate, operating from detailed life plans. They worked—apparently."

They spotted the other ship while still several hours out, the commander making contact with the station as soon as the communications gap had been cut to a manageable few seconds. He came to Karyn and Martin, worried.

"Troopers," he said. "Two hundred and fifty is the complement of a ship that size."

"What are they doing here?"

"They're here to aid the station cadre upon request from the Empire police."

Martin returned with him to the control center, where he contacted the station again. He tried not to be obvious in his questioning but there was no real way to avoid the obvious.

"Do you have a problem?"

"No problems," reported the woman at the duty desk. "We've received a request from Empire Prime to locate a specific transportee. It's a situation we've never seen before—the man was dropped over twenty years ago."

"What man?"

She looked at a stat. "Aaron Caldwell."

"Did Prime say what he's wanted for?"

She shrugged. "Not to me. I must say, it's a pretty puzzle they've set. There are over ten thousand transportees downstairs, scattered to God's heaven and back again. We've located over two hundred separate groupings, but every now and then we lose one—about half of them turn nomadic. But Prime wants this Caldwell, so we dropped a trooper with each group. Most of them have already reported back negative, but it's going to take us the next two weeks to retrieve them all."

Karyn shouldered herself forward, demanded of the woman, "Who ordered the search for Caldwell?"

The duty officer recognized the Empress, for no other face was so familiar to the citizens of the Empire; but she managed to contain her shock.

"The order comes directly from the Council, m'lady—signed by Lord Stennock."

She relaxed then and turned to Martin. "Could he have known that we were trying to rescue Aaron?"

"I don't know. Perhaps. Stennock must have penetrated very close to us. But it doesn't matter now, Karyn—Stennock is gone. You can turn the search to our own advantage."

The station and the troop ship were both out of contact with Earth, had been out of communication since the issuance of the order for there could be no communication without subspace translation. Thus both complements were astonished to discover the presence of the Empress and distrusting of the reported change in the Council. But their loyalty was sworn to the person of Karyn, not to the Council on Earth, and it took little to convince them that Karyn should receive their support now.

Thus it was no problem to switch communications links directly to the station quarters given Karyn, and when the time allotted for contact expired the station began to probe the half-dozen men not yet accounted for. One by one over the next few hours four of them reported in with negatives. The other two troopers could not be contacted at all.

"He must be in one or another of those locations," said the station commander. He did not add the reservation that the others were so wont to use. "Fortunately the drops are in the same general territory. We can cover them both with a single scout ship."

"I want something larger than a scout," said Martin. The party would be large, with himself and Karyn, I'bel and Solomon. The fat man had been Caldwell's closest companion in the days prior to his capture and transportation. It had been their original hope that his presence would help break the wipe conditioning. Now that I'bel had dashed water on that, he felt that he owed the other at least this chance to see his old friend first.

It was necessary to take the gig normally used to drop the transportees on the surface. The pilot asked if they wanted the sleep gas used.

"No," said Martin. "That won't be necessary. The masquerade is over."

The pilot stared a moment, not understanding, then took the ship down. There was room for a dozen in the passenger compartment but Martin had rejected all but their own four plus the commander of their own ship.

They chose right the first time, setting down in the largest grain field just outside the village. Watching on the screens as the locks cycled they could see that their appearance had produced panic in most of the villagers, although the missing troopers were running straight toward the ship—both men here together, for some reason.

And then Martin saw that there were a few, three or four, standing against the apparition. He could tell by the expression on the faces of Karyn and Solomon that Caldwell was one of them.

The troopers were astonished at the appearance of the Empress in the lock, at first refusing to believe their eyes. But Karyn's image had been carried before them all their lives, was prominent in every public place. There was no other who dared look like her; if there was natural resemblance then they employed cosmetics to change.

They were given no chance to report their success for the half-dozen people in the ship were coming out, passing by them, going to the little group still standing in the center of the village. The Empress stopped a dozen paces away and held up her hand.

"Aaron?"

He stared blankly, inured now to marvels by a surfeit of such. He felt that there was nothing more to amaze him ever. He watched the woman who had spoken first, not knowing that she was beautiful, for by the standards of his people beauty lay in a simple line, a soft curve. This stranger in her glittering costume was heavy with artifice.

Then the men who had come with her attracted his attention, first the giant, for he was much the largest man ever seen in the village. Then he was looking at the other man, their eyes meeting, melding.

. . . I know you . . .

Martin staggered against the blow at his mind, then stumbled a pace forward. At the same time Aaron moved also, until they were close enough to touch hands. But they stood there alone.

. . . you were with me in my yesterdays . . .

. . . I told them you were innocent, but they wouldn't listen wouldn't listen wouldn't listen

the time was green that summer when I held her in my arms and we dreamed of you dreamed of what you could be would be . . .

. . . you are . . . I was . . . we will . . .

Minds met, touched, passed each other in a tearing fury that was more than pain, more than love, more than anything could possibly be, an emotion without expression, without which there could be no life, no truth, no touching. . . .

Sky master . . . The scream burst from Aaron's lips at the same moment that it burst from his mind, and there was instant answer, the majestic touch soothing, calming.

. . . it is right . . .

No! I can't stand it!

. . . you must . . . you can . . . you will . . .

"I can't! I cannot do this!"

But minds were meeting, touching, shaping each other as the meld became complete, the two mirror barriers shattering, vanishing as they became one together again in a torrent of emotion and questions and sensation and answers and heart brain liver intestines eyes soul becoming one and forever the same as it had always, would be, and must ever have been.

The two minds met, aided in their contact by the will of the alien race. Aaron became Martin became father became son and together they knew who they were, what they had been, what they must become.

You were my father . . .

I am. I brought you into this world, protected you against my enemies.

But . . . she chose me . . .

No. I chose you, working through her father. I brought

you into the palace. We intended you to marry, but I was taken by the hounds before the arrangements could be finalized. You were our instrument to break the power of the Council.

Stennock is defeated . . .

Cross? Dulange? Profelt?

Dead, years ago, every one of them. Only Stennock was left, and now he has fallen victim to his own instrument. . . .

Then we have won. . . .

Aaron opened his eyes and looked to his Empress. "Karyn . . ."

CHAPTER THIRTEEN

Exhaustion placed Martin in the station clinic for the next seventy-two hours, under deep sedation against the terrible headache that had blinded him when Aaron finally broke contact. At the end of that time the medication was removed and he was allowed to return through the natural levels of sleep to consciousness. He opened his eyes to see Solomon sitting bed-watch.

"You knew," he said.

The fat man's eyes twinkled. "I placed you with the citizen woman who claimed to be your real mother. This is a scheme we've been building a long time, lad."

"Raselle said three generations."

"More," said Solomon. "This fight has been going for all of history, since the first slave master tried to make the first slave. Too many times he succeeded."

"What happens to the Empire?"

Solomon's eyebrows raised. "Why, nothing. What would you have happen? The form of government means nothing—it is the intent of the controlling powers. There have been times and societies in history when democracy was feasible, but how could you give the vote to ten billions, ninety-nine percent of whom have never had the chance to think or do for themselves? No, the citizens don't want the vote—they want the Empire to go on as it has, feeding them and entertaining them and perhaps even loving them."

"Aaron?—my father?"

"He'll answer for himself," said Solomon.

Aaron came with Karyn a few minutes later, as soon as he received word that Martin was awake. He had finally faced the Empress in an uncomfortable interview, after avoiding it for three days.

"I loved you," said Karyn.

"You were in love with the image of a man important to the well-being of your father, whom you really loved." He faced her reluctantly, forcing himself to touch her hand. "I was the power behind the throne. In me you saw the chance to marry your father."

"You make it seem so childish, schoolgirlish."

"You were a child . . . then," he said softly. "Now you are a woman, and strong enough to put away the dreams of a child. Think not of what could never be, but of what can be now that you are Empress in truth."

"I won't hold the power," she said, sulking. "You want it to be in Martin's hands."

Aaron took her hands gently. "Was there ever a man not ruled by the woman he loved?"

———◆———

Now he looked at his son. There was an itch in his spine, for the clothes given him by the station staff were still strange on his back. He had been the object of much study and the subject of many conversations, for he was the first ever to recover from the mind-wipe process. Until then they had believed that the wipe completely removed the memories, the experiences, the learned responses; but it was obvious now that the original personality still remained, buried so deeply that only the most traumatic contact could bring it forth again.

"We'll return to Earth as soon as they let me out of this bed," said Martin.

Aaron shook his head. "I'm not going with you."

"Not going?" He looked at Karyn. "Why?"

"There's nothing for me on Earth. This world has been my home for twenty years. It has been harsh, with only our hands and our brains, but give us aid and we can build the world Earth has not been for five hundred years."

"What about the transportees?"

"Leave them here. They've adjusted to new conditions. Why shatter their lives twice?"

"Can we restore their memories?"

Aaron closed his eyes, let his mind probe out. Even here, so many thousands of miles out from the surface, there was almost instant contact.

. . . *sky-master?*

. . . *man-equal* . . .

"We could restore them, but it would be wrong. They are happy as they are. Those last, who came with you this trip—they do not know this planet. We can restore them to their Earth lives."

Martin accepted his decision. He reached for Aaron's hand, clasped it tightly.

"There is one more I can aid," said Aaron. "The boy, Tomas. Let him stay here with me—there is nothing for him there. I can restore him or not as you wish, but this is his place. I will raise him as my son . . . my son."

Martin was silent a moment; then he said, "Restore him. I want him to know what he was, where he came from. I want him to remember. . . ."

"He will remember you," promised his father.

"Enough sentimentality!" said Solomon with a sudden roar. "Out, both of you—out! It's a long time back to Earth, and I for one have business there that must be taken care of! There are thieves and robbers who have been anxious to take me down for these fifty years, but if I'm bankrupt the bill will go to the royal treasury."

Martin watched them leave. He knew that Aaron was premature in thinking that they had won over all of their opposition just because the enemies he knew twenty years ago were dead. There would always be new enemies, just as there would always be new men. Perhaps the battle was what made life worth living, for Aaron had chosen to continue his war against the forces of this world rather than Earth. But he was still fighting, he would always be fighting.

His son could do no less.